**A YEAR OF SHORT FICTION**

# 2023 STONE'S THROW

**FROM ROCK AND A HARD PLACE**

STONE'S THROW EDITOR: R.D. Sullivan
RHP EDITOR-IN-CHIEF: Roger Nokes
MANAGING EDITOR: Jay Butkowski
CONTRIBUTING EDITOR: Albert Tucher
ASSOCIATE EDITOR: Paul J. Garth
ASSOCIATE EDITOR: Rob D. Smith
GUARDIAN ANGEL: Jonathan Elliott
COVER ART: Heather Garth

ON THE WEB: **www.rockandahard-placemag.com/stones-throw**
ON FACEBOOK: **@RHP_Press**
ON TWITTER: **@RHP_Press**
ON B'SKY: **@rhppress.bsky.social**
BY EMAIL: **editors@rockandahardplacemag.com**

*Rock and a Hard Place Magazine,* our *Stone's Throw* annual collections, and all other works released through RHP Press are a labor of love, produced by a team of volunteer editors to showcase the best in dark fiction, crime, dystopian fiction, and noir. To learn how you can support the mission of **Rock and a Hard Place Press** through tax-deductible donations, or by subscribing to the RHP Patreon, please visit the website, and click "**Support RHP**" through the main menu.

Print ISBN: 979-8-9878765-3-4

eBook ISBN: 979-8-9878765-4-1


Copyright © 2023 by Rock and a Hard Place Press

All rights reserved.

No portion of this book may be reproduced in any form without written permission from the publisher or author, except as permitted by U.S. copyright law.

# Contents

Foreword — 2

1. Kindling Delight — 5
   Joseph S. Walker

2. Crabby Feelings — 11
   Ashley-Ruth M. Bernier

3. Palko — 17
   Nikki Dolson

4. Siren Song — 27
   Francelia Belton

5. The Sand Bar — 35
   M.E. Proctor

6. Shoelaces — 43
   Jonathan Newman

7. Usufructus — 51
   Suze Kay

8. Playing House — 59
   Mary Thorson

| | | |
|---|---|---|
| 9. | Well Beyond Sorry<br>Tom Andes | 67 |
| 10. | Flying Ham<br>Preston Lang | 75 |
| 11. | Pin Bone Stew<br>Aidan Shousky | 83 |
| 12. | Pay the Ferryman<br>Libby Cudmore | 91 |

EDITORIAL BIOGRAPHIES ... 98

# Foreword

How does that *Rent* song go again—"In how many murders do you measure a year?"

Close enough.

*Proud* doesn't quite capture how I feel about this collection of stories. A little over a year ago, this was a loose concept brought to me by the founders of **Rock and a Hard Place**. The whole team then massaged it into something with form, guides and rules, and the stories started pouring in. It was a very Frankenstein's lab moment of seeing the heart of the monster you've built start beating.

I think our pleasure in the project has outlasted the good doctor's, however.

There is something magical in reading stacks of stories, each good in its own right, then coming across The One. The perfect story. The story that, when you reflect on the prompt, swung for the bleachers and knocked it out of the park. The story that sends you scrabbling to talk to the other editors about it.

And to have twelve of those this year, well... consider us very lucky editors.

If you had told me last year I'd spend my 2023 publishing stories of crabs and sirens, of deadly falling meat and murderous stew, I might have asked for a drug screening. For us both. And yet, that's what I'm beyond proud to give you. These authors blew me away with their creativity, ingenuity, and storytelling, and I'm privileged to have worked with them.

I'm privileged as well to work with such an amazing team at **Rock and a Hard Place**. It was always going to be a group effort, producing a story every month, but they made it possible. Every time life came at me and I had to put down a piece of *Stone's Throw*, someone was there, picking it back up and running with it.

And that's how it happens, folks. Writers trust you with their stories, your coworkers help carry the load, and at the end of the year you look up from the grind and see in your wake what you've all done together.

We hope you enjoy this collection of *Stone's Throw* stories as much as we loved publishing them. Here's to a banner first year in the bag, and upping the ante in the years to come.

*-R.D. Sullivan*
*Stone's Throw Editor*
*December, 2023*

**JANUARY 2023 PROMPT** – The beginning of a new year is always seen as a time for personal change. Whether we're casting off old relationships, starting new ones, or just taking up running (from our problems), the goal is to be proactive in making our lives better. But as the road to hell is paved with good intentions, sometimes our attempts to improve our situation just dig our hole a little deeper.

For January's Stone's Throw, your stories don't need to take place on the New Year holiday, but they do need to be about change. Send us your best stories of people trying to change, no matter how ill-advised that change may be.

# Kindling Delight

## Joseph S. Walker

"Look around you," the little Asian lady on TV said. "Contemplate each object in your space carefully. Does it kindle delight? If not, why not set it free?"

I blinked. It was all the answer I could manage.

"Your home is beautiful," the Asian lady told a family, standing in front of a five-foot pile of clothing they'd dragged from every room in the house. "But it has become a place where you merely store things, not a place where you live. By ridding yourself of all that does not kindle delight, you will create space to breathe and be content."

That sounded nice.

I was on the couch in the middle of the morning, my eyes fixed on the big TV mounted to the wall. I was hyperattentive, but completely incapable of movement; aftereffects of whatever brew of booze, pills, and pot I'd subjected myself to in the last twenty-four hours. During a commercial break, I thought hard about my left hand, but couldn't get it to budge.

Uncle Chad had been over the previous night with a bunch of his crew. You don't say no when Uncle Chad offers you a pill, even if you don't know what it is. The last thing I remembered was a couple of his guys getting in a fistfight over a poker game. Seemed like I just blinked and here I was, alone as far as I could tell, captive to the screen.

It was tuned to a cable channel showing a marathon of *Kindling Delight*. In every episode, the woman, Sakura, visited three families who had lost control of the sheer volume of stuff in their homes. One of the couples was always gay or interracial. Sometimes both. Sakura solved their problems, basically, by making them throw a lot of shit out, but before they could toss anything, they had to hold onto it, and think about it, and see if it kindled delight. Then, at the very end, Sakura went back to each family a month or two later, to bask as they thanked her for changing their lives.

At first, I was annoyed by the people Sakura visited. They all lived in beautiful homes, homes like I only saw in real life when I was breaking in while the owners were on vacation, but they would be in tears about a little clutter. I mean, I'm supposed to feel sorry for you because you have too much crap?

I'll be damned, though, if I *didn't* start feeling a little sorry for them by the third episode, and even happy when they felt better. It was the way they acted like completely different people as they stood in emptied-out rooms marveling at their sense of inner peace. They looked like the actual weight had been lifted off them. Hell, they looked younger.

After several hours of Sakura, I couldn't help thinking about the stuff I was surrounded by all the time. Like, take the big cardboard box in the corner to the side of the TV. Uncle Chad stuck it there years ago to throw beer cans into, so they wouldn't be rolling around on the floor. That worked great, except nobody ever cleared out the box. Actually, you couldn't even see the box anymore, but I was pretty sure it was down there, in the base of the mountain of sour-smelling, sticky beer cans crawling up the walls where they met. I didn't think the box kindled delight. It wouldn't have kindled delight even if I could still see it. So I found a roll of trash bags and started shoveling the cans in. I was on the fifth bag before I realized I wasn't paralyzed anymore.

I kept it up for the next few days. Uncle Chad was on a trip down south for some business he didn't tell me about, and nobody else had any reason to come by with him gone. Uncle Chad installed me in the house three or four years back to keep an eye on the trailhead at the back of the property, that led a few miles back to the cabins where his guys cooked. I got to be Uncle Chad's problem when my daddy, his brother, was killed by some Oklahoma bikers who objected to Uncle Chad moving product under their noses.

Sometimes days or weeks passed without anybody coming to the house. Sometimes Uncle Chad stashed stuff there. Sometimes he came by with members of his crew and some women and partied. Sometimes he showed up in the middle of the night and dragged me out to unload a hijacked truck or help beat the shit out of a guy who came up short on a bet.

Uncle Chad dabbled in a lot of lines of work.

The house never really felt like home, so I never really took care of it. Now I did, applying Sakura's test to everything. Aside from some of my clothes, the TV, and my personal supply of weed, hardly anything in the house kindled delight. I hauled bag after bag out to the side of the road to wait for trash day. I couldn't do anything about the broken-down furniture, and I knew better than to mess with Uncle Chad's stuff. He had a big safe in a back room that I didn't have the combination for, several loaded handguns and shotguns under piles of old blankets in the front closet, and a go-bag behind a false back in a kitchen cabinet.

Even leaving all that stuff alone, I got the place looking a lot better pretty quickly.

Smelling better, too. I started to understand the way the people on Sakura's show felt, like I could breathe easier. It was nice to walk from one room into another without immediately seeing some huge mess that would never be taken care of.

That's when I really got to thinking.

If I could make the house better, could I make myself better?

Could *I* kindle delight?

I remembered Uncle Chad at the card table in the dining room, sharpening a knife and smoking a cigar-sized joint, telling a bunch of us about a high school girl who OD'd on some of his junk. Good news, though, he said. She had paid upfront.

Everybody laughed.

I laughed.

I remembered Uncle Chad smashing a guy's fingers in a car door for looking the wrong way at the wrong woman in the wrong bar.

I remembered the way I felt when I visited a guy who owed Uncle Chad money and drove my fist, again and again and again, into the middle of his face.

None of those memories kindled delight. I couldn't think of any that did.

"It's never too late," Sakura always told her families. "The life you want is already here, if you carve away the things you don't."

I was a week into my project when I came back from a walk in the woods and found Uncle Chad on the back deck. He sat in a chair with his long legs stretched out in front of him and watched me come across the yard.

He wasn't drinking or smoking, which was a bad sign.

"What the fuck you done to this place?" he asked when I got close.

I stepped up onto the deck. "Nothing. Cleaning up a little."

"There must be fifty sacks out there by the road. You trying to draw attention?"

"Just got tired of living in filth. That's all."

"That's all, huh?"

"Actually, no." I perched on the arm of the chair facing his. "I'm gonna get my GED. Maybe go to college."

"College." Uncle Chad said the word flatly.

"I can't live like this anymore. I want a real life, a straight life. I want to kindle delight."

Uncle Chad could be hellishly fast when he wanted. I didn't see him move, just felt the back of his hand whip across my face. My head snapped to the side and I went sprawling to the deck. I might have passed out for a second. When I was fully aware again, I was propped up on my elbows and my head felt like the inside of an alarm bell. Uncle Chad was in his chair, still leaning back like nothing had happened.

"You ever talk like that again, I'll tie you to the wall and let the boys take turns beating on you."

I didn't answer. I was moving my jaw gingerly back and forth.

"Now, speaking of college, there's a couple boys been dealing at frat parties without paying tax. You and me are going over tonight to show them the error of their ways. So go wash the blood off your nose, and don't give me no more shit about *delight*."

I picked myself up and went inside. I went straight to the front closet and pushed aside the blankets on the floor. All the guns were loaded. I picked one up at random.

Even a worthless old asshole like Uncle Chad could be turned around, I figured. Even he could kindle delight. All I had to do was turn him into fertilizer.

Flowers kindle delight. I'd plant some beauties on top of him.

**JOSEPH S. WALKER** (Twitter: @JSWalkerAuthor) lives in Indiana and teaches college literature and composition courses. His short fiction has appeared in *Alfred Hitchcock's Mystery Magazine*, *Ellery Queen's Mystery Magazine*, *Mystery Weekly*, *Tough*, and a number of other magazines and anthologies. He has been nominated for the Edgar Award and the Derringer Award and has won the Bill Crider Prize for Short Fiction. He also won the Al Blanchard Award in 2019 and 2021.

**FEBRUARY 2023 PROMPT** — Ah, February means love is in the air! The birds are singing, green is coming back to the plants, and we've let love into our fragile, beating hearts. Now all we can do is hope . . . hope that it stays very, very still and resists tearing free of our chests and casting our love to the still-frozen earth . . .

# Crabby Feelings

## Ashley-Ruth M. Bernier

We all take the creed before we get to the pet shop: our bond with our human, our *one*, comes first. Dogs do it. Cats, too—although much more reluctantly. And yes, even us hermit crabs. You might not be able to tell, but curled up deep in our shells or hidden in our terrarium sand, the truth of that creed courses through our claws and our hairy little legs. That bond is everything. That bond is life.

My Julie made it easy to keep. I knew she was the one the moment she walked into the shop. It had been four weeks of snot-nosed kids glancing at my glass cage and then tearing off toward the puppy section, four weeks of adults who tapped the glass once or twice and then meandered to the fish tanks. Julie was the one who stayed. She was short and slim, with warm brown skin; box braids with a hint of blue plaited into them. She leaned in. Looked into my eyes. Nodded.

"Think I'll call you Shellby," she'd said. Her voice sounded like a day at the beach. *Shellby*. I liked that. I think she knew. She took me away that day. Took me home.

A home in a home in a home. My shell, my decked-out terrarium; our cozy townhouse. Julie played calypso music and read her poems out loud to me. She laughed when I climbed on the mesh cage she bought, and put me on her hand, knowing I'd never pinch her. We were happy.

Or so I thought.

I didn't mind Brett at first. He and Julie met playing baseball together in something called an *adult rec league*. He made her laugh with ridiculous jokes and tried to dance to her music, even though his moves were all wrong. Brett had wrinkled his nose through his catcher's mask the first time Julie showed me to him.

"Kinda puny," he'd said dismissively.

"Oh, come on, Brett. It's not about size, it's about heart," Julie responded. And she believed that. We both did.

It was different after he moved in. He and Julie didn't laugh as much as before. There were arguments that I could never see from my terrarium in the living room but were loud enough for me to hear across the house. Sometimes, Julie cried. She stopped playing music. Her poems lost their hopefulness and light. After a while, she stopped reading them to me altogether.

The biggest change, though, was Claws. I don't know what possessed Brett to forgo flowers or chocolate after one of their big fights and bring home another hermit crab as reconciliation instead.

"We all need someone," he'd said as he dumped Claws onto my sand. "Even your little crab in there, wasting away by itself. Loneliness kills, Julie. You need me here. I need to be here with you. You understand."

"Brett, I don't think we need—" Julie had tried, but he'd cut her off.

"Look, I'm not going anywhere," he'd told her. I remember the words sounding a lot more threatening than reassuring, but I don't remember exactly what Julie said to them. I was too busy eyeing Claws. This wasn't going to work.

Hey, I get it—maybe you've never spent time with hermit crabs before. Maybe you don't know we have actual personalities, just like people do. Claws was big and bombastic. He didn't talk much, but oh, he made his feelings very clear. He barreled over me for food and took up so much space in my Krabby Hut that I could no longer fit inside.

He spent the entire day relaxing in my dipping pool, and if I got there first, he'd threaten me.

"Rip," he'd growl. Claws could only manage one word at a time, but I knew what he meant. A big crab like him could pull me right out of my shell and dismember me in seconds if he wanted to. I gave him my pool and my hut and spent my days curled up in a corner of the cage, wishing he would leave. Wishing they both would.

The day it happened, the fight had been particularly bad. I was the only one around to hear it—Claws, blessedly, had muttered "Molting" to me, and pulled himself out of his shell. He burrowed down in the terrarium sand to shed his exoskeleton, ready to grow even larger. I'd been reacquainting myself with the dipping pool when I heard Julie cry out from the bedroom. A few seconds later, Brett stormed out of the front door with his baseball bag, yelling something about not blaming him—how *this* was all her fault; how *she'd* made him do it.

It seemed like an eternity before she wandered out into the living room to sob on the couch. I scuttled from the pool to get a closer look, and that's when I saw it. The cut on her lip. The bruise on her cheek. The emptiness in her eyes. Something began to burn inside of me. I think—you know, I think it was that *creed*. And I knew exactly what I needed to do.

It was easy to find Claws. He was still sleeping. Still without his shell. Still completely vulnerable. I never could've done it, attacked and pulled him apart like that, if he were awake. If he'd had that protective shell around him. I did feel a pang of remorse as I hauled one of his pincers back to the surface—Claws was, of course, one of my kind—but this was for Julie. If Claws had taken that creed, he would've understood.

I scuttled to the corner of the terrarium and knocked the glass a little bit. It was enough to get her attention. She walked over and leaned in, the way she used to.

"Where's Claws? Oh—Shellby, what happened?" She scooped me up in one hand and pulled up the pieces of Claws with the other. There was a pause. Maybe it was a few seconds, maybe it was longer.

"Did you do this?" She looked into my eyes. I looked back into hers, *telling* her what I'd done. And after a few, she nodded. She understood.

I knew she did. I watched her look it up online. Sometimes crabs attack others when they're out of their protective shell and molting, but *sometimes*, the molting process just goes badly and the crab dies. Sometimes, it's an accident. It's impossible to tell the difference.

The police certainly couldn't, in Brett's case. He'd been taking off his catcher's gear in the doorway in the dark, and he'd just gotten his helmet off when he'd been whacked in the skull with a metal bat. The cops understood—Julie thought she'd been defending herself from an intruder. There were news stories and a trial, just as a formality; but things have settled down now. The house is filled with calypso music again, and Julie reads me her poems while I soak in the dipping pool. They call us 'hermit' crabs, sure, but I agree with Brett on one thing—we all do need someone.

I've got Julie. Our bond is life.

**ASHLEY-RUTH M. BERNIER** (Twitter: @armbernier) lives in Apex, NC. Originally from St. Thomas, U.S. Virgin Islands, she is an emerging writer of contemporary Caribbean mysteries. The winner of the North Carolina Writers Network's 2022 Jacobs/Jones Award for Black writers, Ashley-Ruth's stories have appeared in *Ellery Queen Mystery Magazine*, *Black Cat Weekly*, and *The Caribbean Writer*. Ashley-Ruth is a first-grade teacher and mom of 4, so writing time is more valuable than gold in her house.

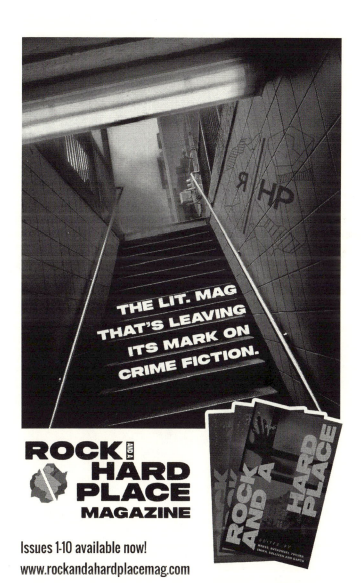

**MARCH 2023 PROMPT** – Organizations are typically pyramid-shaped. You've got one or two guys at the top making the calls and lining their pockets, while the majority of the people form the base. The grunts. The workers. The thugs.

Problem is, they outnumber the rest of the levels. If they ever realize it, that base gets real shaky, real fast . . .

# Palko

## Nikki Dolson

The sound of fireworks going off covered up Palko's gunshots as he killed the men tied up in the house. In the backyard, Jersey watched their exit. Francie was at the sliding glass door, whispering, "Come on Palko. Just leave them." One street over, someone's fireworks went up and exploded blue and green against the moonless night sky. She glanced up at it and felt like a spotlight was on her.

She didn't see him come at her.

Palko grabbed her by the throat and put his gun in her face. "Don't talk to me like I'm one of your kids."

Francie kicked him high on his thigh. He flinched back, dropping his hold on her and lowering the gun.

"We're running out of time."

"I'm tying up loose ends."

Francie shook her head as she walked away from him. Everyone was a loose end to Palko and tonight he was in a mood to hurt people. Better those sorry S.O.B.s than herself or Jersey catching any more of that mood. She crossed the yard to where Jersey stood looking over the six-foot-high wall. She touched his arm and he turned his pale face to her. His nose was still bleeding from where Palko had smacked him in the house because he'd gotten in his way. He hit them. Intimidated them. Blackmailed them. The crew was tired of Palko.

"Your nose is still bleeding."

Jersey wiped at his nose. The sky lit up orange over them. "What's he doing?"

Francie looked back at the house and saw Palko's shadow drift across the closed kitchen curtains. "Whatever he wants. Like always." She tugged the backpack off Jersey's shoulder.

"About that thing? I'm in." A tiny bit of tension left her body. She only had to worry about Mathews now.

Palko came up behind them and grabbed the backpack from her. He unzipped it and pulled out handfuls of baggies from his pockets and placed them into the bag. "The fuck you waiting on? Let's go." He put the backpack on and hopped up and over the wall.

\*\*\*

It'd been six months since the last job. Six months of normal life. Going to work, paying bills, BBQing at someone's house. Their kids playing together. Their spouses and partners commiserating about just how bad Francie, Mathews, and Jersey were about chores around the house, being late or on time. Regular people complaints about schools or doctor visits and the price of insurance. About not having enough and paying through the nose. Jersey's twin daughters started hockey lessons because they didn't want to be figure skaters and his heart was broken because he'd wanted his princesses in tutus but instead, he had princesses in hockey masks. Francie's wife Magdalena had painted butterflies on the girls' goalie masks, making the tips of the wings form into points like fangs. His girls had squealed in delight.

Then two weeks ago, Palko showed up in everyone's life again. He cornered Mathews on a smoke break behind the casino where he dealt cards. Jersey was in his backyard cleaning out the grill for that night's dinner with the crew. Francie had been at the grocery store with Maggie and both kids. Their boys, four and five years old, were bouncing in the cart and singing "wheels on the bus go round and round," and at the end of an aisle was Palko, gesturing for her to come with him.

Palko said some version of the same thing to each of them. "I have a job. We go in ten days." He'd heard that a series of robberies across the valley were done by the same guys. He had a plan to take what they had and make it his own. Palko was smart enough. He was good with numbers, but he was always hungry for the rush, for the money, for the clout. He wanted to be a big player.

To get what he wanted, Palko threatened them if they said no. After all, Jersey's wife didn't know about what he did for extra money. The casino would suspend Mathews if not outright fire him if they knew about his involvement with Palko, and without the union insurance, how could he take care of his mother? And Francie, well, the guys were like family to her. She agreed so they wouldn't get hurt. She sent Maggie and the boys out to California to visit family with the promise she'd be out there to take them to Mouseland, as her kids liked to call it. She kissed the concerned look off Maggie's face. Maggie knew what was going on and didn't like it one bit, but she went. Francie would need a few thousand to take her family on vacation. First though, she had to handle Palko.

\*\*\*

They followed Palko over the backyard wall and down the street. They were dressed in black t-shirts and polyester pants like they were headed to work at some casino. They crossed streets to keep in the dark as much as possible. At the spot where Mathews should've been waiting for them, right in front of the house for sale, he was nowhere to be found.

Palko was swearing. Jersey's eyes were wide and fearful. Francie wanted to scream and pump her fist in the air. Instead, she said, "Stop yelling. It's barely ten o'clock. People are still awake."

"Where the fuck is he?" Palko screamed in her face.

"Maybe he got spooked," Jersey offered. Palko spun on him and Jersey took a step back.

"I don't know where he is, but I'm not sticking around. Come on, Jersey."

"Where are you going?" Palko stepped in her way.

"We have to pay Boone his cut and we can't be here when the cops come, right?" She pitched her voice low and soothing. "So we get to the backup car." He sneered at that. She knew he wanted to ride to Boone's in comfort and style, not in a run-down vehicle with peeling paint. Mathews had a high-end SUV with plush leather seats that he used for the nights he drove rideshare for extra money. Palko liked it when Mathews chauffeured him around.

"You're calling the shots now?"

"It's your plan. I'm just following it."

This seemed to please him. Palko nodded and took point again. They hit Charleston Boulevard, turned right then down a dark alley without a single light to shine upon them or the twenty-year-old black Chevy Impala that would be their ride. Palko had them ditch their guns down a sewer manhole.

Francie had found the vehicle. She knew what it could do and how hard to push it. It looked worn down but the motor purred when she turned the key. Palko slapped the dash. "Let's move."

While she drove, Palko pulled out a roll of black trash bags from the backpack and some rubber bands. He worked for a janitorial supply company and had access to an endless supply of garbage bags. They were his thing. Not a single job happened without him pulling out those bags. He separated the pills into one bag. Into another went the loose diamonds they'd found, along with some watches and rings. Next, he pulled cash out, both bundled and loose. He counted the loose bills and rubber banded stack after stack of them, then counted the bundles.

"How much?" Francie said.

"Enough for today." Whether that was an answer to her question or a commandment to shut up she didn't actually care. Mathews was in.

Oh god, Francie thought, they were really doing this. At a stoplight, she glanced in the rearview mirror and found Jersey's eyes. There was worry in those eyes. She blew out a breath and turned the car onto Desert Inn Road. They cruised up and over the Strip and toward their night's end.

***

It'd been Mathews who'd brought up getting out from under Palko. "I don't know how much longer I can keep going like this." Francie handed him another bolt. They were in Mathews' garage assembling the second of two bikes meant for Jersey's twins. Sweat dripped off his bald head onto the concrete. The garage door was open for some kind of breeze, but it was July and the air was still as a held breath.

"What would you risk to get out?" she said.

He sat back on his heels and looked outside. A skinny kid with locs raised his hand as he went by on a skateboard. Mathews and Francie both waved. "We risk everything every time we go out. I can't do this job. My ma needs me here. I can't go to prison. I can't leave her."

Francie nodded. "I'll figure something out." And she had, though Mathews hadn't liked it much. Too risky he said. She knew he'd probably shake to pieces under the stress of knowing what was waiting for Palko tonight. He couldn't be there. She extracted a promise from Mathews and he kept it. That was step 1. Step 2, take the backup car. Step 3 was next.

***

Twenty minutes later they were down past Boulder Highway turning in at a mobile home park. They drove past rows of small single wide homes with fake flowers in terracotta pots decorating decks and stairs. At the very end was a triple wide. This mansion of the park belonged to Boone and reminded everyone that he was the king of the place. Francie had spent time in that house back when she and Boone had been something more, but that was before Maggie and the kids. Now Francie had a life she was afraid of losing. Boone would understand that. She wanted out. They all did. Everyone but Palko.

Francie parked behind the house. While Boone's security patted the guys down, she slid her hand under the driver's seat and peeled away the gun stashed there. She reached back under for the bag of cash, which she placed under the passenger seat. Inside was ten thousand dollars. They each put the sum together out of savings and piggy banks and items pawned. It had to be enough money to be believable.

Trev patted her down. She knew him from the old days. His pat down was cursory at best. More like he patted the air around her. Trev opened the door for them and Palko led them in.

They were ushered into Boone's kill room. A large room with every surface in it completely covered in plastic. Boone liked to see fear on the faces of the people who stood before him. He rarely killed anyone in it because if you killed everyone who annoyed you, you'd quickly have no one to work for you. Boone was in a brown leather chair at the back of the room. The crew fell into familiar formation, Palko and Francie side by side in front of Boone, Jersey leaned against a wall. Boone's men in the four corners with their guns out. Boone gave Francie a once over and a dimple flashed. He gave off car salesman energy with his slicked back blond hair and dead brown eyes. His gaze fell on Palko.

"So how'd you do?"

"Me and my crew took them down easy. 85k, some pills and some shine." Palko said as he moved slowly forward to lay his offerings at Boone's feet.

"That's not bad. Something to say, sweetness?" Boone was looking at Francie. She'd made a face when Palko had said "my crew." She had dropped it quick but not quick enough. Boone saw everything.

"She doesn't have anything to say, do you Francie?" Palko loomed over her.

She could feel Jersey behind her wondering if she would do what she said. If she could set them free.

"He's shorting you."

There was a beat of silence then Palko exploded. "The fuck I am."

Francie dodged his first swing but caught an elbow from the second and hit the floor. Boone was out of his chair and his men were on Palko, holding him back.

"Any truth to that?" Boone asked Jersey.

Jersey kept his head down. "I didn't see anything from the backseat but if Francie says it's true, why wouldn't it be?"

"They're lying," Palko spat.

"Check under the passenger seat," Francie said as she got up.

Boone returned to his seat and waved his men away. They let go of Palko. "Don't touch her again."

Palko seethed but didn't move. Trev went to check the car and returned with the cash in the same kind of black trash bag that Palko had put before Boone.

Palko's jaw went slack. "You know I wouldn't."

Boone looked at Francie.

"I bet he brought the job to you, didn't he? Made big promises about what was there and how much he could bring you, but does this line up with that?" Francie gestured at the bags. "We aren't going down for his greed. We have too much to lose."

"This is a set-up. You lying bitch. Boone, you know it was you—"

Boone held up his hand. "What should I do about it, Francie? This sounds like a crew problem. Should've sorted this issue before you walked in here."

"I'll sort her and she'll be back inside five minutes begging to tell you the truth." Palko took a step toward her. Francie reached into her pocket and pulled out the gun. She aimed low and shot him in the knee. Palko went down screaming. Blood spattered the floor. Boone was up again, his arms outstretched to hold off his men.

Jersey took the gun from her. His hand shook as he pointed the gun at Palko. Francie put her hand on Jersey's shoulder to steady him as he shot Palko in the stomach. Palko wailed. She took the gun back and looked down at him. Blood was on his lips and hate and anger and disbelief rippled across his face.

"We aren't your crew," Francie said, then shot Palko in the head.

\*\*\*

Later, as his men wrapped up Palko's body, Boone said to her, "Thing is, I contacted Palko about this job. Not the other way around."

Francie shrugged. "He was stealing from you."

"I knew that but I got enough from him. Price of doing business sometimes."

"If he was stealing from you, he was stealing from us. It had to be done. You keep your percentage, and the ten grand for your trouble, plus the jewelry, and pills."

Boone rubbed his chin. "Doesn't seem like enough money for all your trouble though."

"It's plenty. And Palko had to go."

**NIKKI DOLSON** (Twitter: @nikkidolson) is the author of the novel *All Things Violent* and the story collection *Love and Other Criminal Behavior*. Her stories have appeared in *Vautrin*, *TriQuarterly*, *Tough*, *ThugLit*, and other publications. Her fiction has been nominated for a Derringer and selected for *Best American Mystery and Suspense 2021*. You can find her at nikkidolson.com.

*Rock and a Hard Place Press Presents:*

# UNDER THE THUMB
## STORIES OF POLICE OPPRESSION
### Guest-Edited by S.A. Cosby

In this anthology, we explore the darker side of the badge, where a traffic stop can go one of two ways: bad or worse. Where evidence can and will be forged. Where the Blue Wall of Silence closes ranks, and accountability becomes a four-letter word.

Is the system broken? Or are we meant to live our lives *Under The Thumb*?

### Nominated for a 2022 Anthony Award for Best Anthology

### With stories by:
Travis Wade Beaty, Andrew Case, Hilary Davidson, Hector Duarte, Jr., Michael Downing, Jeffrey Eaton, Michael A. Gonzales, James D.F. Hannah, Zakariah Johnson, Preston Lang, Bobby Mathews, Mike McHone, Richie Narvaez, Oluseyi Onabanjo, James Queally, Keith Rosson, Jeff Soloway, Joseph S. Walker, and Tim P. Walker.

**WHAT READERS ARE SAYING:**

"Powerful Voices with a Serious Message"

"Hits Like a Nightstick to the Gut"

"A Blistering Collection -- Recommended"

**WWW.ROCKANDAHARDPLACEMAG.COM/UNDER-THE-THUMB**

**APRIL 2023 PROMPT** – Lust is a powerful motivator. It's fond of grabbing our hearts and masquerading as love, until everything lays around us in ruins. When all is unmasked, we find our thinking had been done by hormones, and what we did in the name of hormones can't be as easily undone.

For April, give us your stories of love and lust gone awry, of people swayed by a pretty face and prettier words.

There's a reason a rabbit is the mascot of Spring . . .

# Siren Song

## Francelia Belton

I told him he was my Brandy, like that 70s song from the Looking Glass, the one you like. I said that to all the guys I slept with. And he believed me, 'cause you know, I'm a sailor.

There aren't many of us women who sail the seas. The captain of my own ship, I run a private international moving company. Took over the business after my father died. But you know that.

Was I promiscuous? Maybe. Still, I'd proven my nautical worth. I did what I wanted. How I wanted. And no one could take that from me.

So I told him he was my Brandy. It worked. It was the 80s; the song was popular and made a great pickup line. Corny, I know. Nevertheless, men ate it up.

I think most men considered me a challenge: *reel in the sea loving mariner, tame her, and make her your wife* sort of thing. Only that's not how it works. You can't 'domesticate' a seafarer. They love the salty wind in their hair, the cool water against their skin, the sound of the waves crashing against the hull of their ship. When I told men they were my Brandy, they never understood. Not really. There was no happy ending for Brandy. She wasn't able to draw the sailor in with her feminine wiles. She just wasted her life waiting.

And I can say for a fact that no man could net me with his 'masculine' charms, either.

And yet with this guy . . . it was different.

I actually meant it when I called him that. I mean, there were so many similarities between our story and the lyrics. First, his name was Brandon, which wasn't very common for a Black man back then. And I met him in a harbor town. Seaport Village. A facsimile of a harbor town, but close enough.

It was 1980, and the opening weekend of this San Diego tourist attraction. I had pulled into Point Loma Marina the night before and had a few days before my next shipment.

I strolled through the outdoor mall, contemplating dining at one of the many restaurants, or popping into one of the shops to peruse the overpriced wares. Nibbling on cotton candy, I passed artists drawing caricature portraits of teenage lovebirds, while little kids begged their parents for a balloon animal from silly clowns.

The guitar playing is what first captured my attention. I rounded the corner and saw the man who was playing my siren song. He was tall and lean, with curly black hair and eyes that truly could 'steal' me from the sea. They were vivid green, another unique quality for someone of color, and contrasted strikingly against the deep walnut brown of his skin. Much darker than my own medium brown. As I walked up to him, I noticed he had long black lashes. He didn't sing while playing the guitar, merely smiled to himself as if there was a secret that only he alone knew about.

I wanted to find out what it was.

I spent the rest of the day sitting at the park listening to him play, and talking with him when he took his breaks. Many people walked by, some spending a few minutes listening, some dropping dollar bills into his guitar case.

So yeah, I liked Brandon. Did I love him? Probably. Maybe. I was close, anyway. However, one thing about the Brandy song was definitely true: the sea did call to me. The sea was my love, my life, and most importantly, my livelihood. A philosophy I learned from my father. He drilled into me: "Business comes first. Before love, before family, before anything. Because in our line of business, if you don't take care of it, it will take care of you." And I never deviated from it. Flings were one thing. In different cities and countries and ports. Never seeing any of them more than twice. I couldn't afford to get attached or have any of them get attached to me.

My mother tried to trap my father by getting pregnant with me. She thought she could lure him in from the sea permanently. But she was wrong. Instead, she lost her life, and my father raised me to learn the business. Most importantly of all, to love the sea before anything else.

Except, I broke my own rule, and I saw Brandon more than I should have.

At first, the arrangement was fine. Brandon had other women, and I was off doing my thing at sea. We had agreed what we had was a casual fling. I would see him when my travels brought me to San Diego, meeting at Seaport Village, then spending the weekend in bed at the Westgate Hotel.

I always brought him gifts, beautiful things from exotic places. A fine Italian leather wallet from Florence. An authentic African mask from Ghana. And yes, even the requisite silver chain from the "North of Spain," Castro Urdiales' finest. Instead of my name in a locket, I gave him a pendant in the shape of the letter B made out of emeralds. Eventually, my gifts were not enough to appease him. He wanted more.

He just couldn't understand—or didn't want to understand.

He began asking questions.

*What exactly did I do?* I told him I was in the shipping business, which was true.

*Why couldn't he see my ship?* Because it was a private business with upscale clientele who demanded strict confidentiality. I made that clear in the very beginning.

However, the question he always asked the most was, *am I in love with someone else?* I reminded him I don't fall in love.

We were spending too much time together, even with long lulls in between my visits. Yet I couldn't help myself. I was . . . hooked.

And then, the day I knew would come finally arrived. Brandon told me he was fed up. He was not like Brandy in the song. He wasn't content to wait.

Maybe I should have taken his discontent seriously. Or maybe I should have broken it off then, but seafarers know the strength of a tide, and once again, I found myself back in Seaport Village.

On my last and final visit to San Diego, 19 years to this day actually, I brought Brandon a custom-built Ovation Balladeer guitar. I knew he'd always dreamed of one, and I wanted to see him happy one last time. Unfortunately, he wasn't happy with it. What he wanted was me. He wanted us to be together. I told him this is the best I could do, take it or leave it. He took the guitar and left, and when he was gone, I was sure I'd never see him again.

But I was wrong.

I'd forgotten he was as drawn to me as I was to him, and though I didn't see him, he followed me to my ship, where he saw everything I'd tried to keep away from him. He saw my crew loading merchandise that would never go through customs or be cleared by any port authority. He even saw some of my clients.

When my clients had gone, Brandon confronted me. Only not in the way you would have expected. He wasn't mad. Wasn't disappointed. He didn't feel lied to. Instead, he told me he wanted to be a part of it. I wouldn't have to hide myself anymore. We could be together. No more secrets. He'd go out to sea with me. "I'll follow you anywhere," he'd said.

I like to think of myself as a practical woman. Imaginative enough to envision all scenarios and my possible reactions to them, but I never saw this one. This wasn't how the song went. Brandy always wanted the *sailor* to give up the waves. But I could actually have both. Brandon and the sea.

Letting Brandon think I was excited by the prospect, I encouraged him to go home to pack his belongings. However, from the moment he'd suggested a new life together, I'd known the idea was doomed. I didn't run a legitimate business. I dealt in international smuggling and with all kinds of shady characters. If any one of them found out who and what Brandon meant to me . . . he would become a liability.

After a few hours, Brandon came back with a few bags and the guitar I bought him. I said nothing because I didn't want to spoil the mood. But the fear of what would happen to us if we were found out was on my mind as I steered the ship out to sea.

In deep water now, I stood at the stern of the ship, looking at the moon and stars reflecting off the ocean waves.

Brandon came up from behind and wrapped his arms around me. He whispered that our story was better than the Brandy song. We were getting our happy ending.

The waves rocked, and underneath them, I heard the song. Not Brandy, but the song I'd heard my whole life. The tide was changing. Pulling back. Drowning out the love I felt for him.

Sailors know it's one thing to see a lover every two to three months, but it's quite another to be around them day in and day out. Brandon was needy. He would always be in my hair. And I knew he would miss his life. He wanted to play his guitar to crowds, to maybe even record an album. He wouldn't be able to do that with me.

I reached under the boat's main panel, then turned in his arms as the tears ran down my face.

He was smiling when I stabbed him in the heart with the stiletto.

His eyes widened with shock and confusion. But it was the hurt on his face that pierced my soul.

His body grew heavy in my arms, and I stepped back, holding him and whispered, "There are no such things as happy endings," just before I pushed him overboard.

My crew was loyal. Each of them felt the song too. Each of them knew, without me having to explain. One of them cleaned the blood from the deck, while another pitched Brandon's bags into the sea.

Though not Brandon's guitar, not right away. I held onto the Balladeer for a while, plucking a few of his favorite chords before casting it in the ocean, which was calm that evening.

The instrument made the last sound it would ever make—a disharmonious splash as it hit the water.

I watched it sink, a part of me submerging with it. I couldn't keep it, even though I wanted to. Even though I knew the guitar had its own song.

I didn't find out about you until later.

That's why your name is Brandi Rose, after me and your father. And where you get your pretty green eyes and curly hair from him. And that pendant you're touching. Yes, it was his.

Now you know why we never dock in San Diego when we come to California. Too many memories for me. Even so, I promised I would show you where I met your father. And I'm a woman of my word.

See that palm tree over there? It was at that bench. He was playing his guitar under the fronds.

His song was so beautiful.

He was so beautiful.

You told me your boyfriend plays the sax, right? I can see why you like that about him. I guess music is in your blood, too.

Now, you can run away with this boy if you want to, but you gotta ask yourself if you'll really be happy. Because no matter what you tell yourself, the sea is in your blood. Just like it was for my father. Just like it is for me.

It never fades away.

Your father was the only man I considered giving up the sea for.

But in the end, the sea always wins.

**FRANCELIA BELTON's** (Twitter: @FranceliaBelton) love of short stories came from watching old *Twilight Zone* and *Alfred Hitchcock Presents* television shows in her youth. She published a collection titled, *Crime & Passion: Three Short Stories*, and her fiction has appeared in various publications, including ""Dreaming of Ella"" in *Denver Noir* and ""Red Riding in the Hood"" in *Bizarre Bazaar*.

Her short story, "Knife Girl," was a finalist in the 2020-2021 ScreenCraft Cinematic Short Story Competition and a semi-finalist in the 2021 Outstanding Screenplays Shorts Competition. Her short story, "The Brotherhood of Tricks and Tricks" was a quarterfinalist in the 2022 ScreenCraft Cinematic Short Story Competition.

She is an active member of Sisters in Crime and has served as President (2019-2021) and Vice President (2015-2018) for the Colorado chapter. She is also a member of Mystery Writers of America, Crime Writers of Color and Short Mystery Fiction Society.

You can read more of her stories at https://Francel.Be/Writing-Stories.

**MAY 2023 PROMPT** – Family—We can't choose them, and we can't choose what they bring to our lives. Whether they have our backs, need our help, or make our lives worse, they're still our blood. From the overbearing parent to the blindly devoted spouse to the judgmental sibling, we want stories befitting RHP that feature family.

Be it blood or chosen family, tell us a story of lives complicated by or with family.

# The Sand Bar

## M.E. Proctor

Try driving from Miami International Airport to Key West in bumper-to-bumper traffic, temps in the mid-nineties, with a three-year-old in the back singing *Baby Shark do do, do do* . . . on repeat. It would push a Zen Master to murder, or send him to holy forbearance.

You either strangle the toddler, or reach beatitude.

Carolyn, my daughter, piece of my heart.

When we park in front of my in-laws' seaside villa, Laura and I are ragged, tempers strung on gossamer threads. Grampa Ollie and Gramma Sharon swoop down on the SUV and release Carolyn, who's still yelling *Baby Shark* at the top of her capacious lungs.

They cluck. "She's so cute. Come, baby, come see your room. It has dolphins."

Dolphins. Is there another song with dolphins that will saw through my nerves?

Laura elbows me in the ribs. "Flipper," she says. "Click click click. Click click." She whistles. "Three hours of that and I'll be ripe for the straitjacket."

"That's CIA hardcore, *Manchurian Candidate*. Knock me out if you see my eyes glaze over and I start saying things like: Got. To. Find. A. Telephone."

She laughs.

"I love you, Lau." I kiss the top of her head.

We offload our bags and Caro's gear. As always, it looks like we've packed for an intergalactic trip instead of a week at the beach.

The kid doesn't care about cooling off and settling in. As soon as she's in her bathing suit, she runs along the deck, screaming to get on the boat. She wears the pink life vest with the characters from *Frozen* that Gramma Sharon bought at the local beach store. Laura follows behind, slathering her with sunscreen. Caro wriggles free, slick as an eel, as soon as the last dab is applied.

"How is she in the water?" Grampa Ollie says.

"She floats."

My father-in-law shoots me a disgusted look. Seven years married and he hasn't warmed to my sense of humor.

"We're taking the boat out, feel free to join." He tramples down toward the dock.

Laura, hands sticky with SPF 50,000, catches the exchange. "You managed to pinch Dad's gills already? We just arrived. That must be a record."

"Your father branded me an asshole the first time he saw me. How long before he asks you, *again*, why you married me?"

"I wish you would try to humor him, Jack. You like running your nails over the blackboard, don't you?"

It *is* entertaining. Oliver Jenkins is easy to rile. He used to run an engineering firm and bossed around a few dozen employees for over thirty years. The habit is tough to break. Anybody who doesn't meet his standard of riding crop subservience is a punk, a hippie, or a hooligan. Words I'm sure he mumbles under his breath each time he looks at me. I'm a criminal attorney. I could tell him a thing or two about punks and their grim lives. And what they're willing to do to get ahead. They're a world away from Ollie, his boat, and his beach.

"You mind if I skip the boat ride, Lau? A book, a cold drink in the shade. I need to chill."

She kisses me. "Promise you won't check email the moment I turn my back."

She knows me well.

Fifteen minutes later, the boat roars away from the dock, Captain Ollie at the helm, ballcap glued to his head. He's showing off for my benefit, with his killer wake rocking the lichen-encrusted pilings. The moment the boat rounds the point, I'm in the sitting room, studying the bar. It looks like a tequila day, and I fix a big ice cube-loaded Paloma. I grab my tablet and scan emails. There isn't much, a couple of questions that I answer quick-fire. It appeases my conscience and I make a beeline to the pool.

Can't say I suffer from being alone in paradise.

Then it's time for another cocktail and my book. And dozing off.

"Daddy, Daddy!"

Caro's voice drills through a comfy dream pillow. She sounds less shrill in this environment than at home, maybe because she harmonizes with the screech of the seagulls.

She jumps in my lap, seawater-soaked, and I help her out of the life vest.

"Dolphins," she yells in my ear. "Sooo many!" Her arms flap like a desynchronized synchronized swimmer. "Everywhere!"

"Looks like you had a good time." I stand up with her wrapped around my neck. "Want to rinse in the pool, punkin?"

"Yessss."

I wish she knew how to control her volume level. She's stuck on 11, like the guys from *Spinal Tap*. Laura walks up carrying a bunch of wet towels. "Okay if I dunk her, Lau?"

She nods. There's something in her face I don't like. Her parents are still on the dock. I can't hear them, but it looks like a nasty argument.

"We swim, Daddyyyy . . ."

Laura drops the towels and rushes inside. My daughter is punching my shoulders.

"You want to float on your back?" I say. "You remember how?"

I stand in the pool next to her, ready to give her a supporting hand, but she's fine, eyes closed, quiet and relaxed, finally.

"Do a dog paddle."

She dips low a couple of times, but the gulps of water don't faze her. She'll be swimming soon. I float on my back next to her and she climbs on top of me. We've done this often, since she saw the video of the otters carrying their babies this way. We go around the pool a few times and she's half asleep by the time the grandparents come back to the house and I'm ready to get out.

"She's a real water baby," Gramma Sharon says.

Ollie groans. He's munching on a thick cigar and looks even more irritated with me than usual. I hand Caro over to Sharon and go check on Laura.

She's in our room, on the bed. Her eyes are red, she's been crying. I take her in my arms.

"What's going on?"

The tears start again and she buries her head in my shoulder.

"Is it your damn father? Did he say something? I swear I'll knock him on his fat ass." The more she cries, the angrier I get. "Goddammit, Laura..."

She puts a cold hand on my mouth to shut me up.

"It isn't Dad... I got so scared, Jack..."

She lets out an anguished moan. I pull her close. "Are you hurt?"

"No. No. Oh, God." She wipes off the tears. "It wasn't dolphins swimming around the boat, Jack. It was sharks. I've never been so scared in my life."

I've only seen a large group of sharks once. In the Caribbean, on a snorkel tour, the guides dropped chum to attract nurse sharks. Inoffensive, they said. It made me want to leap out of the water.

"We were around the point. By the sand bar. Where we always go to swim."

Ollie and Sharon's favorite spot. Clear water, white sand. Colorful little fish that tickle your legs, and the occasional turtle. I never saw anything bigger than a turtle.

"One moment, I was playing with Caro on the tube, and the next the sea was full of them. I had just the time to hand Caro to Mom and grab the ladder." She runs her fingers through her wet hair. "I wanted to scream and I couldn't. I was terrified, and I didn't want to scare Caro . . . God, Jack, it was horrible."

I hold her tight.

"The water turned red. They were . . . frantic. They were biting each other."

"Shhh . . . You're okay. You're all okay." I like the seaside but I'm a landlubber. I'll never pretend I know the sea or understand it. "What did Ollie say?"

"Nothing. He said nothing. He started the boat and we raced back home. Jack?"

"Yeah, baby. It's all right now." I feel so dumb, inept. I was sipping tequila and snoozing, while my wife and daughter were attacked by sharks.

"They shredded the tube."

Her eyes are too big for her face. Pupils reduced to pinpoints of terror.

"I'll get us on a plane tomorrow," I say.

She hesitates. "I don't know . . . Caro won't understand." She shakes her head. "We can't do that to Mom and Dad. It isn't their fault. We don't have to go near the water."

"And when you look at the ocean, you'll see what?"

"I won't look at the water." She has that mulish expression I know well. Like Caro when she refuses to eat what's put in front of her.

***

Caro is with Sharon in the kitchen. I find Ollie on the patio with a scotch and another stinky cigar. He's leaning on the balustrade, eyes on the blue horizon. It gets my hackles up.

"What have you got to say?"

He shrugs. "It's nature."

"Was there a carcass on that sand bar? Something attracted the sharks, Ollie." He argued with Sharon on the dock. What the hell did he do? "Did you drop fish guts? Is that it? You thought it would be fun to show a bunch of frenzied sharks to my daughter?"

He rises to his full height—I have a couple of inches on him—and roars. "You think I'd do a stupid thing like that?"

Frankly, yes, I think he would. But his outrage is real. "Then what is it? You know these waters. What the fuck happened?"

He drops in a cane chair. He doesn't look at me. "I don't know."

I know evasion when I see it. "You must have an idea."

He sighs. "There was an incident, a week ago. A boat sank, with migrants, at night. The Coasties found the wreck; there wasn't much left, couldn't tell how many people went in the drink." He runs a liver-spotted hand through his thin hair—the same gesture as Laura's, and my heart jumps. "There were a lot of sharks still in the area." He looks up at me, pleading. "That was off Marathon, miles from here."

"Did you call the Coast Guards?" I say.

"Why would I?" He looks puzzled.

"Because something brought the sharks there." I hand him my phone. "Call them. Give them the position of the sand bar."

He fights me, it's his nature. "I didn't see any debris worth a damn. Pieces of driftwood, whatever. I can't call the Coasties for nothing. And this is Key West. The Chamber of Commerce . . ."

"Don't give me that *Amity Beach* bullshit. It didn't work in the movie, and it won't work here either. If you don't call them, I will. Laura will talk to them."

He grumbles. He slaps my phone away and gets his: a flip phone, for chrissake.

"Uh, yes? Oliver Jenkins here. I'd like to report an incident? Uh . . . a shark incident."

I leave him to spin his tale. He can pretend to be civic-minded Ollie. He'll have to dodge his Chamber of Commerce buddies. Tourists, sharks, and migrants in flimsy boats do not mix well.

Laura and Sharon are in the kitchen. Caro is sprawled on the rug in front of the fireplace. She digs into a box of toys. Her tablet is on the coffee table, discarded. There's a stack of wooden building bricks that might have belonged to Laura. I plonk down on the rug, with my back to the coffee table. I'm a firm believer in out of sight, out of mind.

"Let's build a house," I say.

Tonight, I'll figure out how to block that damn *Baby Shark* video.

\*\*\*

Migrants in small boats are very much in the news two days later. Thirty-one Cubans beached their raft on a Key Largo beach in front of surprised tourists. The Cubans told the Coast Guards that they lost track of two other boats that left at the same time they did. Searches are ongoing.

Sharks teem in the hundred-mile-wide corridor between the Keys and Cuba. They have ravenous appetites.

**M.E. PROCTOR** (Twitter: @MEProctor3) is currently writing a series of contemporary detective novels. The first book *Street Song* comes out from TouchPoint Press in 2023. Her short stories have been published in *Vautrin*, *Bristol Noir*, *Pulp Modern*, *Mystery Tribune*, *Reckon Review*, *Shotgun Honey* and others. She lives in Livingston, Texas. Website: www.shawmystery.com

**JUNE 2023 PROMPT** — The twenty-first of June is the summer solstice, the longest day of the year. But our longest days (or nights) aren't measured by minutes but by worry, hardship, or struggle. We've all had days like that, where it feels as if hours have passed only to see a couple minutes have vanished off the clock. So to honor the solstice, we want stories about somebody's longest, unending day.

Send us tales of what someone is going through that is making every minute, every second, tick by in the most agonizing way.

# Shoelaces

## Jonathan Newman

The old man would rise early and have no idea where he was. He would sit at the foot of his bed and blink himself into something resembling consciousness, never remembering when the previous day had ended. He would reach for the curtains and allow the sunlight to pour into his small bedroom and close his eyes and enjoy the feel of the light just for a few moments before he forgot all over again. He would sit at the foot of his bed and look down at his bare feet dangling a few inches above the floor. His body was hunched and curved and dwarfish in stature; his feet no longer even grazed the ground when he began his endless days. His fat stomach protruded. His breath rattled. A pair of shoes sat next to his bed, and the old man would look at them for what felt like a long time, and still, he had no idea what they were for.

He would frown and think and screw up his face and shake his head and even cry at the loss of a memory that he knew he had once possessed. He remembered, possibly, his Mama used to do the same, and he would search for her in his memory, the days bleeding together like spilt wine.

Each morning his tears and his movements would bring a visitor to his room. There was always a gentle rap, and the young man would enter. He would speak to the old man as though he knew him, but the old man could only stare. The young man would take the clothes from the chair and would help the old man from his bed, and he would help the old man to dress. Neither said much. The young man pulled the old man's body where it needed to go and slipped each item of clothing on with the care of a friend. The old man would just stare at the younger man and try to remember him. When all that remained was the shoes, the young man would sit the older man back down on the bed and he would crouch down to push the shoes back onto those old feet. Each day when the young man crouched, his shirt would rise, and the old man would see the pistol and the badge, and the young man would see those grey eyes looking and he would shake his head and tell him not to worry.

They would go downstairs and eat breakfast. Sometimes other young men would join them, and sometimes even young women; the old man preferred it when there were young women, but he never remembered that. They would eat toast or pancakes or cereal. They would drink coffee and orange juice, and sometimes the young man would let the old man slip a drop of whiskey into his coffee and then put his finger to his lips and wink. But the old man never remembered, so what difference did it make?

They would do nothing all day. The old man would wander out onto the porch and see he was at a farmhouse in the middle of the desert; he would gaze all around him at the gasping desert and he would be happy just for a few moments before he forgot and sat in the rocking chair on the porch. He would read the newspaper and forget; he would read books and fall asleep. Sometimes the young man or one of his even younger or prettier friends would bring the old man an old, weathered radio and the old man would listen to sports. Only sports. They didn't like the old man listening to the news. Sports was the only way he could tell what time it was during the day. The old man never cared. He never remembered.

This day was different. The sportscaster had said that it was June 21st, baseball season, but the old man had forgotten that by the time he had brushed his teeth, the desert grit staining his teeth. There was a crease to the young man's smile that the old man suspected was probably always there and he just couldn't remember, but he knew he didn't like it. They went downstairs and dined together in silence until the vehicles arrived. More young men entered. It was breezy outside, and the wind flapped and lifted the men's shirts and the old man saw the pistols and the badges. The young men huddled together in the front yard and spoke in voices of low hush that the old man was unable to decipher. He sat on the porch and frowned and enjoyed the feel of the sun. There was sand in his shoes and he did not know why. The men had arrived in a large truck. The old man stared at it and decided that he did not like it.

The young man came over to him and smiled. "Time to go."

"Where we goin'?"

"New place," said the young man. "You'll like it."

"We ain't stayin' here?"

"No, sir," said the young man, draping a jacket over the old man's shoulders.

"I like it here."

"You only been here a day."

"What?"

The young man smiled. "Hands."

The old man held out his hands and the young man snapped on a pair of handcuffs.

"What're those for?" said the old man.

"Protection."

"Whose?"

Winking, the young man led him over to the truck. The back was open, but the old man still balked and hesitated at the doors. He looked like a mule fearing the darkness ahead. The young man spoke in his ear and calmed him and walked with him up the small ramp and into the back of the truck. He slid back the cage door and sat the old man on the chair inside and took his wrists and fastened the handcuffs to the seat and then did the same with the seatbelt.

"Am I dangerous?" said the old man.

"Why d'you ask?"

"You're chainin' me," said the old man. "Did I do somethin' bad? I can't remember. This day . . . all my days . . . I can't remember . . ."

The young man placed a hand on the old man's face and smiled and told him not to worry then stepped out of the cage and closed and locked the door. The old man felt tiny inside those bars; he looked tiny. He felt like an animal and didn't know why this was happening to him. The sun was lost to him. Wind and sand pounded at the side of the van. His days stretched off into an endlessness of despair. He started to cry but something in the back of his mind forced him to stop and suck down his breath and grit his teeth and close his eyes as the doors were closed and the engine rumbled into life and the truck drove him away into the desert and confusion and nothingness.

They drove for what felt like an eternity and yet the old man forgot every second of it. The truck would bump and roll and growl over the hard earth of wherever they were, and the old man would be shaken from side to side. Sometimes the young man, seated just outside the cage with two others, would ask him if he was okay, and the old man would nod and look away and have no idea who he was. Sometimes the young man would pound his fist against the roof of the truck and yell for the driver to slow down or take it easy.

In what could have been the tenth hour or the tenth second of the journey, the brakes slammed on and the old man and everyone else in the back of the truck, blind to the outside world, was tossed around like toys in a child's satchel. The vehicle stopped and the old man watched the young man reach up to strike the roof once more.

And then the gunfire began.

The old man felt the truck lurch and heard glass shattering and the cries of men dying and the sound of bullets ripping through the air and the metallic raindrop as those bullets struck the vehicle in which he cowered.

He remembered, then. Combat and wars in jungles. But his hands were old, this couldn't be *that*, couldn't be *then*, couldn't be *now*.

The rear doors of the truck exploded, and the smoke and sunlight and sand poured in and blinded the old man. He blinked. Held his ears. Focused on his shoes on the floor until he could see. The old man looked through the smoke and saw the young man's face pressed up against the bars of the cage; his eyes were wide and staring, but there was no life in his body, and he slid away from the bars. The falling body reminded the old man of something from his childhood, but what...

The smoke and sand stung his eyes but outside the gunfire ceased and the old man heard more voices but could not understand them. He looked over towards the blasted door and the smoke and the searing sunlight and saw a glimpse of a highway and then a shadow blocked it out.

A man entered the truck, climbing out of the smoke, and walked toward the old man. Two more shadows followed, and the old man looked down. He saw that one of his laces was undone and he realised that he couldn't remember how to tie them.

Keys rattled, and the first figure unlocked the cage door and walked inside, smiling at the old man.

"Hola," he said, kneeling to unfasten the old man's chains.

The old man said nothing but stared at the face until he felt he was free of his shackles. He allowed the man to help him out of his chair and lead him through the back of the truck, stepping through the fallen youth at his feet. The old man held his head high and refused to look down; yet the air stank of death. He was passed down from the back of the truck into the waiting arms of others and he emerged into the sunlight and saw that he was indeed in the middle of a highway, and he squinted into the vastness all around him and saw the smoke and the bullet casings and the blood and the fallen bodies steaming in the sand.

Three pairs of eyes surrounded him.

"Hola," said one.

"Who're you?" said the old man.

The man who had freed him from his chains was the last to jump down from the van. He said something in Spanish. The man leaned in and whispered to the old man. A story from his past. A story they'd both been in. But then the wind blew and the memory was gone, just dust caught in a storm.

The first man took a step backwards and the other two followed.

The old man had nothing to say. The three men backed away towards where a brown pickup was parked at the side of the road. There were bullet casings on the ground and holes in its windshield. They climbed inside and the one in the baseball cap turned to wave back at the old man, and then the truck turned back onto the highway and drove towards the setting sun, leaving the old man shivering and alone.

The old man started to cry. He looked down and saw that now both of his shoes were untied, and he could not remember how to tie them. Ahead of him was an endless highway, a brooding, festering desert, stretching on forever.

The old man bent, removing his shoes, then began to walk, the asphalt scorching his feet.

**JONATHAN NEWMAN** (Twitter: @TheHudsonLives) is an unpublished British writer and long-suffering English teacher. He spends most of his days attempting (unsuccessfully) to convince his students that reading Cormac McCarthy and Stephen King are more valuable interests than using TikTok and Snapchat.

**ON SALE NOW FROM**

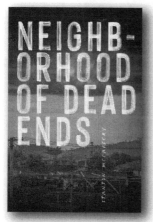

*The latest novel from RHP Editor Stanton McCaffery!*

### WHAT THEY'RE SAYING ...

"Heartbreaking yet fast-paced, Neighborhood of Dead Ends is a gripping story that will stay with you for a long time."
  - Jen Conley (*Seven Ways to Get Rid of Harry*)

"*Dead Ends* is a definite page turner."
  - Charlie Stella (*Johnny Porno* and *Tommy Red*)

"Stanton McCaffery is the king of corruption, despair, and, most importantly, kicking back against the pricks."
  - Ben Whitmer (*Pike* and *Cry Father*)

WWW.ROCKANDAHARDPLACEMAG.COM/NEIGHBORHOOD-OF-DEAD-ENDS

**JULY 2023 PROMPT** – Freedom, in any sense, is rarely obtained without a struggle. From illness to interpersonal drama to all-out war, the object a person chooses freedom from sets the level of conflict encountered. And freedom itself, though touted in this country in a jingoistic sense, is much broader in ways we seek it than the American definition allows.

We can seek freedom from any number of things—relationships, work environments, addiction, incarceration, even simply expectations.

Help us celebrate this July in true RHP fashion, by sending us stories of characters engaged in personal bids for a freedom they desire. What happens when they get it? And can they ever truly be free?

# Usufructus

## Suze Kay

Morgan takes the call on the porch.

"How is he today?" Renee's voice is tinny and pinched over the phone. Morgan can't tell if that's because of emotion or the shit service she gets out here in the bayou.

"It'll be soon." She stares at the scummy green water below and wishes it were clean. When she was a child, she swam in there. She and Renee. When the algae clung to their hair, Mom called it a *mermaid dye job*.

"Long day at the salon, ladies?" she'd say in the outdoor shower, sudsing up their scalps. They'd giggle, imagining a swamp mermaid salon. Morgan looks at the shower now: badly weathered, door off its hinges. No one's used it in years. No one's swum in the water for years either, not since the Robichaux girl got sick from it.

"You said you couldn't make it, but . . ."

"You know I can't." Renee sounds even fainter, and Morgan knows it's not cell service that's dimming her. She remembers how Morgan got on the phone when she cried in high school. She held the phone inches from her ear, as though struggling to hear the boy breaking up with her or the friend telling lies on her would make it all go away. "I'm sorry," she moans. "It kills me to ask you for this. It kills me that I can't be there."

"You'll make it for the funeral, though, right?"

"Yeah, of course." Her voice comes through clear again, all business. "Make sure you send me a copy of the death certificate as soon as you get it, so I can take time off."

***

The house is muggy. Swamp air doesn't have boundaries, it wafts in through windows and doorways; it rises through the floorboards. Edna sits, languid on the musty couch.

"I think he done shit hisself," she says. "Stinks in there."

Morgan rolls her eyes and walks down the dark hallway. All the windows in his room are open, but the pervasive smell still overwhelms her. He whimpers as she changes his diaper, settling again when she pulls the blanket up over his sunken chest. His eyes never open. The blanket is clammy with humidity under her touch, but his skin is hot and dry as paper. The fever is rising again. She hopes it takes him.

Not for the first time, she looks at the bottle of morphine on the dresser.

It would be so easy. He wouldn't exist anymore. Morgan could leave the bayou. Renee could pay off her loans. Then they'd all be free.

***

He passes that night, without her help. Morgan lays on the bed beside him and feels the furnace-like heat of him for the last time. His face tightens when she strokes his forehead, and she can't tell if she's helping or hurting. She does it again. Edna stands in the doorway. His breathing slows, rattling terribly in his chest. It stops.

"He's gone?" Edna asks. Morgan sits up and blinks tears out from her eyes. She presses shaking fingers to his neck and nods. "I'll go make the calls, then."

Morgan lays back down. She whispers all the things she wasn't brave enough to say before into his ear until it's cold and the hospice nurse arrives. After the funeral home takes him, she changes the sheets and offers the master bed to Edna.

"Nah, I'll take Renee's room again. Gives me the heebie-jeebies, thinking of sleeping where he passed."

Morgan sleeps there. She dreams that he sits on the edge of the bed and tells her he's here to give her the heebie-jeebies, and all the fruits thereof. She wakes in the gray-green dawn with gritty eyes and a jaw ache from grinding her teeth all night.

\*\*\*

*I have some bad news*, Renee's text reads. *I just can't do it. I can't go back.* Morgan calls her but can't hear her on the other line. Like she's whispering through a tin can on string, she hears only the vaguest mumble of regret.

"Renee, if you're not going to fucking show up, you need to at least tell it to me straight. Hold the phone to your goddamn mouth for once."

"I CAN'T!" she screams. Morgan almost drops her cell. "Don't you get that?"

"Then what? I have to do it all? I have to stay here by myself? You promised. You said I could leave when he died. You promised me we could sell the house and I could leave."

"I can't talk to you when you're like this. I'll be there on Zoom for the reading of the will. Just calm down. We'll figure it out after that."

Morgan hangs up on her sister. Walking into the house, she slams the screen door so hard it rattles on its hinges. Edna's in the kitchen, pouring herself a dram of his nice scotch.

"Trouble in paradise?" she croons. It's clear this tipple isn't her first of the day.

"You could at least pretend to be sad."

"It's not like he was my husband."

"Yeah, and you know why. Then he couldn't have lived here in my mother's house."

"I always wanted him to leave. Move into the condo with me," she sniffs. The condo is up in Houma, left to her by one of her previous husbands. "This place is a shithole."

"Then go home, Edna."

"I'll stay on for a little while. Be a comfort to you, and so forth." She takes her drink to the porch, leaving the bottle open and Morgan fuming.

***

"To my daughters," the lawyer reads, "I leave my earthly belongings, including the truck and the boat. Go fast. I leave the money in my accounts, and the contents of the safe deposit box at Houma Republic, to them as well. To my beloved Edna, I leave the house on the bayou and a lump sum of $10,000."

"No, that's not right," Renee interjects from the laptop. "The house was held by him in usufruct. It was our mother's. When she died, it was his until death or remarriage. Now it's ours."

The lawyer raises his eyebrows and looks at Edna, who's fanning herself with exaggerated bashfulness. "Well, that's something we can unravel in due time. What it says here is that Ms. Edna Layton gets the house. You two get the belongings and the money. It seems perfectly fair to me."

The air conditioner in the legal office is working overtime, keeping the pristine room so cold Morgan thinks ice wouldn't melt. She shivers in her thin cotton dress. Her mouth feels dry as she asks him when the will was made.

"May 16th, just about two months ago."

"Are you kidding me?" Renee shrieks. "He could barely talk on the phone at that point. Who witnessed it?"

"Myself and Ms. Layton. I assure you he was of sound mind."

"This is a farce. You'll be hearing from our lawyer." In her apartment half a continent away, Renee slams her laptop shut. A descending two-note tone announces her departure to the chilly office.

"Well, I never," Edna drawls. She paddles the fan briskly before her, pushing bedraggled curls this way and that.

\*\*\*

Renee's voice pours through the truck's speaker, ranting about Edna's duplicity, his stupidity.

"I don't want to fight anymore," Morgan feels herself reverting to a long-forgotten childhood avatar, that of the whiny younger sister. Too tired to play. "Why can't we just let her have it?"

"It wasn't his to give," she seethes. "He was only the usufructuary. That house was Mom's. That house was always supposed to be ours. You really want shitty Edna to have it?"

"Renee, you aren't here. Do you know how bad it is? It's falling apart around me. The swamp stinks like shit and dead meat. You can't even fish in the water anymore. It's not worth anything."

"Everything's worth something. You said it's falling apart? Take pictures. If it's really bad, we can make a claim against the money he left her."

"If you want pictures, come take them yourself." She hangs up.

Back in the house, she sits on his bed. The room has finally lost the sour smell of sickness. Now it reeks, like everything else, of swamp and mildew. She googles *usufruct Louisiana* and reads until her eyes hurt. She must fall asleep at some point because he comes back. He looms over her on the bed and tells her that there are no fruits left: the fish are dead, and the alligators are angry. The heebie-jeebies are all, and they shouldn't be hers.

Edna announces her return with a wheezy slam of the screen door. Morgan rubs sleep out of her eyes and goes to meet her.

"You can't make me leave," Edna says. She pulls the scotch back out and pours herself a glass.

"I'm not trying to." Morgan is exhausted. Renee should be here to have this fight.

"He said this house was mine," Edna says. She pours one for Morgan, too.

"Did I say he didn't?"

"Well, your sister certainly thinks I'm a liar. You two have no idea what it's like. Loving people who die. Being what's leftover."

"Why are you so awful? I loved him too, you know." Even as she says it, she isn't sure if it's true. Edna takes a sip of her scotch. His scotch.

"Could've fooled me. Never called, never wrote. All he did was talk about you two, and you didn't even show up until he couldn't say it to your face. Ms. High-and-Mighty didn't show up at all."

"You don't know anything." She takes her scotch and leaves the kitchen. At the doorway, she turns and says, "You don't know anything about what happened in this house."

\*\*\*

That night, he crawls over her like he used to. She freezes and pretends it's not happening here, it's not happening to her, like she used to.

"I'm trying to set you free, you stupid bitch," he whispers, hot in her ear. "I'm trying to say sorry and let you go."

When she wakes up, gasping, she calls Renee. Renee picks up, still half asleep.

"Let her have the fucking house," Morgan sobs. "Why would you even want to own this place? You can't even come back here. You made me come instead. For me, please. Just let it go."

"I don't want him to win." For once, Renee is audible. "I don't want him to take this from us, too."

"I'm leaving in the morning. You can do what you want, but I'm leaving and I'm not coming back, and I'm not going to help you with this."

\*\*\*

On her way out of town, in his truck, with his boat on a trailer, she stops at Houma Republic to look in the safety deposit box. Inside is her mother's jewelry, some pictures, and a letter. *Girls*, it reads, *I left the house to Edna. I took out a loan on it, and I don't want it to be yours to deal with. Let her have it.*

*It won't make up for what I did. I'm sorry. I pretended I didn't know what I was doing, and I lied. Take the money and leave.*

Morgan puts the jewelry in her purse, then chooses some of the photos to take as well. Just the good ones.

She takes a picture of the letter for Renee but leaves it in the box, where she hopes it stays forever.

And then she follows her father's instructions for the last time, and leaves.

**SUZE KAY** graduated from Yale with a degree in Art History. She currently works as a pastry chef in New Jersey and writes short fiction, horror, and fantasy. You can find more of her writing on Vocal Media.

**AUGUST 2023 PROMPT** – Summer stands for a lot of things—vacations, days at the lake, suntans and picnics. It's every kid's school-time daydream and outdoor enthusiast's favorite time of year. But summer also brings heat. Temperatures rise, tempers rise, people crowd together and test each other's patience.

You add enough heat to anything, you get a fire.

For this sizzling summer special of the 'Throw, send us your best story of a situation hitting a boiling point. We want to read about the straw that breaks the camel's back, that last degree that starts the fire burning.

# Playing House

## Mary Thorson

Let's play pretend. I'll get the good china set out, and you run to the store and grab some soda.

"Beer?" you ask.

But I've only ever had sips before from the half-empty bottles my folks leave out around the house. It never tasted so good. It was always warm and flat and sour.

"It's better when it's cold. I'll show you. We'll keep it on ice."

But the icebox is outside. I don't think I want to go outside, yet.

"I'll go, then."

That's nice.

I pull out the china from the built-in cabinet in the dining room. The doors stick because we never ever opened them. Mama got them from her first wedding with Daddy–from Daddy's mama. Then Mama kicked Daddy out. She changed the locks on the doors and he didn't try very hard to get past that inconvenience. She never used them, but she didn't want to sell them.

They are covered in dust, now. They are just covered in dust so thick that when I drag my finger in the shape of a heart on a dinner plate, it cakes instead of gathers. A dark-gray thick smudge instead of seeing white bone underneath. Mama should have cleaned these from time to time.

I set the table for two. Two dinner plates, two little plates, and then the cheap nickel forks and knives that look like a play set my baby sister uses. But when I think about that I feel funny, so I don't think about it, and I don't touch them anymore. They are all cold and stiff.

"What are we gonna eat?" you ask, in a kind of way that doesn't remind me of my stepdaddy and I smile a little. You're real good at making me smile. I won't forget that.

I tell you to check the fridge. Maybe there is something in there. I hope there is because I don't want to tell you. I don't want to spoil anything, but I ain't much of a cook. My Mama kept us out of the kitchen to keep herself sane, she'd always tell us. She'd always yell it. She was always too loud.

"Meatloaf? Looks bad though."

You show it to me. Your black leather jacket bunches around your shoulders as you cradle this small glass pan in your dirty hands. I peek. With my own fingers–my pink painted nails that now are all chipped and broken, I touch it. The ketchup hardened into an ugly crusted zig-zag over the top. There is one slice taken out. Unless Mama split that up and meant for the baby to have one half for dinner now and one half for dinner tomorrow. But I don't want to think about that. I don't mean to think about what the baby's mouth looks like now.

"You see the mold?" you ask.

I do. Some blue and white fuzz sprouting off the ground beef. You scrunch up your face and it looks strange. You look ugly, and my stomach turns a little. I tell you to just cut that part off and heat it up in the oven.

"Really? That's alright?"

Why wouldn't it be?

"I won't get sick?"

No, I say. But I think I don't know what gets you sick.

"How long should I put it in?"

I don't know so I say an hour. I tell you to twist the egg timer all the way around.

"Alright," you say, and you are so unsure that it makes me feel sorry for you–in a bad way. My cheeks get hot. I think we shouldn't have done this. But we didn't do nothing.

You turn around and disappear into the kitchen. We haven't cleaned the kitchen good enough, I suspect, so I don't follow you in there. I picture it all hard and crusted over the linoleum floor or the yellow counters. I don't know where it all got, I make myself think. I make myself think I might not even know it's there.

I walk back into the dining room. It looks dirty because the curtains are all closed and the little light getting in makes everything kind of brown. Dirty and dark. The table has two big plates, two small plates, two knives, and two forks. But I'm wrong. I can't see so good in the dark. There are five big plates, five small plates, five knives, and five forks. And a shotgun. The baby is playing with it, I think. She's picking it up and dropping it, making a bad sound, like one of those pop-up boxes that's meant to scare you. Mama is gripping her butter knife–but I think it's a butcher knife. She knocks it against the table, making another bad sound. They're all so loud–except my stepdaddy. He's quiet. He's got something he's trying to get out of his throat. You come into the dining room like a dog following me.

"What do you want to do while we wait?" you ask.

I think you mean to try something with me. Something physical. I see that your face has a smile on it that I've seen before. A look you get when you're about to hit someone for no reason. I like that look. I take your hand, and before I lead you upstairs, I look, again, at the table. They're all still there, but you don't see them. They're all still making noise, but you don't hear them. Mama, in particular, looks real mad. She hates you.

The stairs creak and the baby's room is right at the top. The door is open. I ask you to close it, even though she's not in there. Maybe she is–maybe I don't know. I take you past Mama's room and through the side of my eye I can see the covers piled up in the middle of the bed, I can almost think she's taking a nap. She's just waiting for Betty Jean to wake up. And scream and scream because mama moves too slow like she can't hear it and that child has a set of lungs on it that reach down and wring your spine with crazy sound. But that's alright. She's quiet now, and you and I can be secret.

We get to my room. It's small. All the things in it look like someone else's now. I don't know why. I get sad, real sad all of a sudden, because I guess I know we can't stay here very long. Even I know people won't think we all have the flu forever. Mama's work is gonna call. School is gonna call. They'll send the truancy officer down and we'd be dumber than rocks to be answering the door. I sniffle, because I want you to know I'm sad.

"Darling," you say, just like I planned on you saying, but now it doesn't sound the same.

"You know I'll take care of everything, right? You know I will," you say. And maybe you will. Maybe we can leave and get ourselves a nice little house away from all the pigs and chickens and shit where we put them—no no no no no, where you put them. Where I don't know. Mama is sleeping. Betty Jean is sleeping. My stepdaddy is working or maybe he's even being real quiet out in the shed because he's laying face down on that thin wood board that shouldn't even be able to hold his fat ass, as all the chickens hop around his quiet self.

From my room, I can hear them chickens. They're upset that they've been disturbed.

"Come sit next to me." You're on my bed now. You pat my yellow daisy quilt with your dirty hand. I come over. I sit down and your weight in the bed makes me lean towards you when I'm not sure that's what I want to do. But you don't do nothing, really. You put your hand on my back and start rubbing it. But then I kiss you so we can get this done.

Later, we walk back down the hall to the stairs, passing my still-sleeping mama and my still-sleeping sister. What time is it? How long have they been asleep? It's a little darker in the house. You're a little disappointed. I'm a little glad it's over. I walk in front of you so I don't have to contend with the way your shoulders slouch. The bottom of the stairs looks completely black. Like maybe there isn't even a floor there anymore. But, even if I'm scared of the dark, I'll keep walking, because I smell something burning.

"What is that?" you ask.

It's the meatloaf, dummy. I run into the kitchen. I turn on the light but I shouldn't have. I should have thought. I should have fumbled in the dark and burned my own hands instead. But I'm just as dumb as you because I am so surprised when the light comes on and shows everything we missed. I can't shut my eyes, but I want to. You charge ahead and open up the stove and smoke floats out across the room, and I still see everything. There are bits of mama's hair on the walls like spaghetti noodles.

"It's all black," you say, but her hair is red.

Scrape it off. It ain't burned all the way through, there's something in the middle there that's good. There's got to be. Before you can say anything, I get out of there. I go back to the dining room. They're all still there. They're all still waiting. Mama has her knife ready. Betty Jean has the butt of the shotgun in her mouth, working her gums around it because she's teething. You come in and you still don't see them. You put the meatloaf in the middle of the table. Mama bangs her butcher knife when your hand gets close to her. She wants to stick you with it so bad, but she can't because you were stronger. Stepdaddy wants to scream and holler at you, but he can't because you gave him such a surprise. And Betty Jean is only looking at me but she don't know no better, because I don't know a thing.

**MARY THORSON** (Twitter: @MaryThorson6429) lives and writes in Milwaukee, Wisconsin. She received her BA in Creative Writing from the University of Wisconsin-Milwaukee and her MFA from Pacific University in Oregon. Her stories have appeared in the *Los Angeles Review*, *Milwaukee Noir*, *Worcester Review*, **Rock and a Hard Place**, *Tough*, among others. Her work has been nominated for *Best American Short Stories*, *Best American Mystery*, a Derringer, and a Pushcart Prize. She hangs out with her two daughters, husband, and dog when she isn't teaching high school English, reading, or writing ghost stories.

The New Anthology from
Rock and a Hard Place Press

# THE ONE PERCENT:
### TALES OF THE SUPER WEALTHY AND DEPRAVED

*The One Percent* exposes the obscenely rich for what they are: a symptom of an economic system gone off the rails, and in some cases, the cause.

Greedy and vampiric, they have polluted our waters, raped our land, and profited from untold amounts of spilled blood.

And that's before we even get into the dick-shaped rocket ships.

## 16 STORIES DETAILING THE MOST VILE OF THE MOST PRIVILEGED FROM:

C.W. Blackwell, Scott Von Doviak, Esther Mubawa, James D.F. Hannah, AD Schweiss, Thomas Trang, Meirav Devash, Eddie McNamara, Andrew Rucker Jones, Sam Wiebe, Curtis Ippolito, Tim P. Walker, Jesse Lee, Sean Logan, Tom Andes, Steven-Eliot Altman, and Lin Morris.

WWW.ROCKANDAHARDPLACEMAG.COM/THE-ONE-PERCENT

**SEPTEMBER 2023 PROMPT** — It's the little things that happen every day, the ones we don't think about. Sometimes it's an accidental shoulder bump on the bus. Other times it's a shopping cart collision, a parking spot dispute, accidentally cutting in line. Small things that are inconsequential moments in our lives. What happens, however, when it's a bigger deal to the other person? When their notoriety, infamy, celebrity grants them a sense of entitlement you violated?

The theme of this month is Trip into Fall, and we want your stories of a tiny mistake having major, perhaps fatal, consequences.

# Well Beyond Sorry

Tom Andes

It started with a bump, brushing the guy's shoulder as they passed through customs in Arrivals at Gatwick, and sure, maybe Derrick had leaned into it, not wanting to give ground, not wanting to cede territory to a guy wearing a suit that looked like it cost more than Derrick had in checking and savings combined. But he'd just gotten off a six-hour flight from Boston, and he was tired. And his head was swimming, thinking about Karen's long legs, her big brown eyes, her smile.

And anyway, it was just a bump.

*Fucking American prick*, the guy said. Derrick was pretty sure he'd heard that over the noise of *Siamese Dream* in his headphones. And yeah, that baseball cap was a dead giveaway that he was a Yank. And he knew how people felt about Americans overseas, especially with that whole situation in the Persian Gulf a couple years back, which Derrick wasn't going to pretend to understand, so he didn't have an opinion about it.

But he was a homer, a lifelong Red Sox fan. His grandpa had given him that cap a few weeks before the old guy died, and Derrick never left Boston without it, not even when he was going to London to see his smoking hot Argentine girlfriend, Karen, who was waiting for him in her family's apartment near Hyde Park Corner, which they were going to have to themselves for a week.

And anyway, it wasn't more than a bump, and that should've been the end of that.

But the guy was waiting for him outside the terminal, and Derrick felt like he'd stepped into that scene in *The Long Good Friday* where they stuff Bob Hoskins in a car, a pre-*Remington Steele* Pierce Brosnan turns around in the front, and you know the Hoskins character is going to die.

It was absurd, like so stupid, man.

One minute Derrick was coming out the doors, trying to figure out where to catch the train, realizing he had to go back inside to get to the station, and the next minute this guy was standing in front of him, all of like five-four, shoes spit-shined, in a blue custom-tailored suit, wearing so much fancy-ass cologne he was probably a fire hazard, a faint smell of mint or maybe it was tea tree oil, from the toothpick he was chewing.

"You should watch where you're going."

"Might say the same thing to you," Derrick said, "buddy."

"I'm not your buddy." And the guy bumped Derrick's chest, shoving him back a step on the sidewalk.

"What's your problem, man?"

"You ran into me." The guy was breathing hard, his nostrils flared, a day's growth of stubble on his face, with a fierce-looking blackhead on his chin. "That's my problem. Man."

He said this last in a broad, flat Yankee accent, *taking the piss*—wasn't that what these Brits said?—and now that Derrick was closer to the guy, if he had it to do over, maybe he would've stepped out of his way. Dude's neck was thick, scar tissue and a few white slashes like checkmarks through his eyebrows, like he'd once been a fighter or at least taken a few shots to the face.

Derrick's grandpa had been a fighter. The old guy had shown Derrick a few moves: he could handle himself.

Music was clattering from the headphones around Derrick's neck.

"You could've stepped out of the way," Derrick said, "too."

And now the guy was touching him, mashing the pudgy tip of a forefinger into Derrick's chest like he was putting out a cigar.

"Tell me," the guy said, "that you're sorry."

Derrick started laughing.

Right, that's all it would take to defuse the situation, and it seemed so easy.

And he might've done it, too.

But what if Karen was watching? Karen, the super-hot, blonde, Argentine International Relations major he'd met last semester as an exchange student, who'd invited him to stay with her for a week. If Derrick was a solid seven, she was a 10, and he couldn't believe his luck. And he couldn't get it out of his head, what she might think of him backing down.

"All it'll take," Derrick said, "is me saying sorry?"

He didn't want to say it, not with the Karen in his head watching, not even if she wasn't the kind of chick who went in for stupid displays of machismo. Not even if he wasn't a macho dude. Not even if it was the smart play, and the sooner he got past this chump, the sooner he'd be at Karen's flat.

"All it'll take," the guy said, "if you do it now."

And Derrick was about to do it.

He just had to choke down a big old chunk of pride.

Now the guy was grinning, showing a gap between his front teeth.

"And you have to get on your knees when you say it, mate."

The guy wasn't going to throw down, not on the curb in front of International Arrivals at Gatwick at 11:00 on a Tuesday morning, with all the, what-did-you-call-them, lorries driving past, and those black cabs, one of which was waiting at the curb, its door open, tailpipe chugging.

And anyway, it was just a bump.

"Out of my way." Derrick shouldered past the guy, not caring this time that he was the one who'd initiated the contact, even though the check he gave would get you whistled playing ice hockey like he'd done growing up.

*Mate*, he called the guy, putting a little stank on it.

\*\*\*

He couldn't say how he ended up in the car.

One minute he was walking past this dude in his thousand-dollar suit, looking up at the blue sky, thinking about how good a shower would feel when he got to Karen's place, and the next minute his arm was jacked up behind his back, until he felt something give, maybe tendon, maybe bone. And the minute after that, he was in the backseat of that cab that had been idling at the curb, with his right arm dangling at his side, that psychotic dude he'd bumped into back in the terminal sitting in the jump seat across from him.

A man with slicked black hair was driving. For one disorienting second, Derrick almost gave the cabbie Karen's address in Mayfair. Then the pain hit him.

"You dislocated my shoulder."

The guy was looking out the window, scratching his chin, thoughtful, like he was considering what Derrick had said. As they left the airport, fields rolled past, maybe the same ones he'd seen from the plane, rape, and linseed blooming purple and gold, like in that song by Sting. This couldn't be happening. He closed his eyes, tried to wish himself back to the airport terminal, but he was still in that car, the pain in his shoulder too much to ignore.

"I think there's been a mistake."

"There's definitely been a mistake."

"I'm sorry, man. There, I said it. Isn't that what you want to hear?"

"I think this has gone well beyond sorry, mate."

Years ago, when Derrick had played left wing for his high school team, this big Canuck had checked him into the boards and popped his right shoulder out of its socket. Now, gritting his teeth, he reached behind his head, grabbing his opposite elbow with his good arm and pulling, until, with a sickening scrape of bone and cartilage, the arm popped back into place. Retching, he leaned forward with his head between his knees. Bile dripped onto the floor of the cab.

"Fuck's sake." Glancing over his shoulder, the driver swerved.

The guy in the suit said, "He's just lucky he didn't puke on my shoe, isn't he?"

And he flicked his toe in the direction of Derrick's nose as if to kick him in the face, so Derrick flinched, covering up.

"Just make sure he don't shit himself," the driver said. "I don't want to have to clean some bloody Yank's piss and shite out the back of me cab."

Derrick's stomach dropped, a cold feeling working its way through his intestines. Next to him on the seat was his green Army surplus duffel. His headphones were still around his neck, the music coming from them tinny and distant, Billy Corgan singing "Today is the greatest day I've ever known."

Karen loved that song. She'd turned him onto Smashing Pumpkins, Radiohead, Massive Attack, half the stuff he listened to that was cool that year. A society girl, an ambassador's daughter, she had the best taste and the cash to drop on whatever music she wanted.

Maybe he was never going to see her again.

"Look, man, I'm sorry I bumped you. I guess I was kind of an asshole about it, and I'm sorry for that, too. But it was just a bump. I didn't mean it."

"He still doesn't get it," the cabbie said, "does he?"

"No," the guy said. "He doesn't get it at all."

Sometimes Karen talked about the other men in her life, including a guy who wanted to marry her in London, a real gangster type, she'd said, part of that fast crowd she ran with, and it made Derrick jealous, sure. But she was her own woman, a free spirit, nothing was going to hold her down, and she made it sound light and fun, like they were just dating, maybe holding hands and going out for ice cream. Anyway, what could Derrick say, since they weren't exclusive, and there was that whole issue of citizenship and the fact they lived across an ocean?

"Is this about Karen?"

Something was behind the guy's smile. For the first time, he looked uncertain, his chin balled, that blackhead ready to pop.

No one in the world knew where Derrick was right now—not his mom, not Karen—no one except these two men in that cab. His grandpa who'd taught him how to throw a punch and take care of himself had been dead five years.

"You shouldn't go picking someone else's peaches," the guy said, "if it's not your tree."

"But they're not your peaches. And it's not your tree."

"Not yours, either."

"It wasn't anything between us except a little fun, anyway. It isn't serious."

"It isn't serious?"

"Yeah, it isn't serious."

"This," the guy said, "is serious."

They were driving through the outskirts of London, one of those red double-decker busses boxing them into a roundabout, and Derrick let himself hope this was a joke, that these guys were going to drop him at Karen's, or maybe back at Gatwick, where he could hop the first flight home, like the coward he was. At a stoplight, across from a pub called The Red Lion, he lunged for the door, yanked the handle.

"Locked," the guy said, "from the front."

"What do you want from me?" Derrick said.

"Maybe I want you to open that bag, pull a hundred thousand quid out."

Shaking, Derrick knelt in the back of the cab. Thank God Karen wasn't here to see him beg for his life. "Please." But the guy was laughing.

As the sun broke through the gloom, they turned toward the South Downs, leaving London behind, heading into those green, rolling hills.

"No." With his thumb, the guy brushed a tear from Derrick's cheek. "This isn't going to be that easy, mate."

**TOM ANDES'** (Twitter: @thomaseandes) writing has appeared in *Best American Mystery Stories 2012*. He won the 2019 Gold Medal for Best Novel-in-Progress from the Pirate's Alley Faulkner Society. He released his debut EP, "Static on Every Station" on Bandcamp in 2022.

**OCTOBER 2023 PROMPT** – Anyone who grew up with the Internet can tell you—it's forever. It's the most striking example of the ghosts of our pasts coming back to change our lives now, but it's bigger than an errant tweet. It's the Golden State Killer being caught through a family member's DNA profile. It's women decades away from an employer finding the strength to finally tell their stories of abuse and harassment.

For October, the epitome of spooky, we want your best story of the skeletons in your character's closet, literal or metaphorical, finally seeing the light of day. Tell us what haunts them, and what they intend to do about it.

# Flying Ham

## Preston Lang

Comas are expensive. Owen had been in his and on his back for almost thirteen years. None of the caregivers wanted to boot him out of the facility, but Glenda constantly received bright red notices and phone calls from desk monkeys a thousand miles away—*we feel we've been more than compassionate with you*. She couldn't begin to cover the debts, and every month just piled on more. Still, she came early every day and read to her husband, held his hand and told him about the world. She'd start with the good things, the Crocuses and Robins and other signs that spring was coming, but she'd end up complaining, spitting curses at everything wrong and rotten.

They had been on the interstate, about thirty miles from home, when the canned ham hit the windshield and the car plowed into the concrete of the high overpass. Glenda came out of it with a two-inch gash on her left forearm, but 128 ounces of cured meat, packed inside aluminum, thrown from 43 feet up had ended Owen's waking life.

At first, she'd been hot for revenge. A man driving a minivan told police he thought he saw a boy in a hoodie running off after the crash. Glenda hounded the detectives. *Have you talked to local schools?* She wanted a list of all troubled boys within a fifty-mile radius. Bring them to the station and grill them one by one. But the useless police wouldn't do this, so she'd taken to driving by middle schools, watching kids in the yard, hoping some little motion in the way a boy threw a football or dumped his lunch in the trash would signal his guilt. But it never did, and Owen needed her—a comatose man requires a constant advocate. She gave up.

Years passed without a word or voluntary movement. She'd now known Owen much longer this way than as someone who could walk, or discuss Shakira, or tell her she had spinach in her teeth. No one expected him to come out of it, but no one could say definitively that he wouldn't.

And, of course, it was hilarious. A canned ham. A popular comedian worked up an extended bit about the accident. A year later, his HBO special was called *Flying Ham*. The ads showed him standing haplessly while a rocket-powered can shot toward his head. It was just the kind of cosmic buffoonery he was known for—*so I gotta look out for terrorists, colon cancer, and now flying ham?*

Glenda had watched the routine many times, usually on her phone right next to Owen. She listened to the laughter and thought of the life she'd lost: getting her Masters, working as a pharmacist, playing tennis, having a child. Instead she spent hours on the phone arguing with insurance companies or begging charitable foundations for money—*Yes, we are appreciative of what you have done for us, but there are so many expenses we haven't been able to meet.*

One Tuesday morning she checked Seed4Life, an online donation platform. The account had gone from 218 dollars to 1.9 million overnight. An instant solution to all her money woes. She called to make sure it wasn't a mistake. The money was verified: an anonymous corporate donation. Seed4Life wouldn't even give her a hint, but when Glenda asked if she could come to their office in Philadelphia to thank the Seed4Life team in person, they had no objections.

Glenda had taken days off before. Not many, but a few trips out of town had been necessary over the years, so the nurses were only a little surprised when she told them she'd be gone a day or two. The earliest bus to Philadelphia got her in before lunch. The Seed4Life office was full of hip, young women, typing, talking on phones. They laughed and leaned back in chairs and threw paper at each other.

Computer terminals were set up all over the office, including two near the windows past the bathroom that no one seemed to use.

The hardest part for Glenda was shaking hands and smiling. People hugged her and told her how lucky she was, but then on the other hand, she was also very unlucky. While Glenda nodded and accepted banalities, a slender woman in cutoff shorts came back to her desk and logged onto her computer. Glenda made sure to move in close enough to see the username and password.

The CEO, Dr. Weiss, had a cluttered office in the back. She was surprisingly spiritual.

"You never know where blessings will come from," Dr. Weiss said.

"No, you certainly do not."

*Sometimes they seem to hit you right out of the sky.*

A letter opener sat on the desk between them, and Glenda picked it up. Years ago, she'd gone on TV with two other coma spouses to raise awareness. Glenda thought awareness was just a euphemism for money, but everyone else wanted to talk about blessings and beauty. It was all she could do to keep from strangling someone on air.

She put down the letter opener.

"Can you tell me where the ladies' room is?"

After Glenda came out of the bathroom, she hit one of the computers, logged in, and quickly found Seed4Life's donor spreadsheet. It took two pages of scrolling to spot her money: a grant from something called CPI Industries with an address in Manhattan. It had been founded four years earlier by a whiz kid named Jeff Trent. He'd graduated high school in California, but there was no information on where he'd gone to middle school. At age seventeen, he'd patented a process that helped promote healing in certain kinds of damaged blood vessels. He chose not to enforce the patent, so one of the big pharma companies took the idea and made all the money. But he'd had other breakthroughs that were just as good. A few years later, he dropped out of a PHD program and started his own research facility. Not yet 26, Trent had built CPI into a company worth 650 million.

It was hard to find pictures of him. He wasn't one of those young millionaires who liked to strut around and make noise, but you can't run a 650-million-dollar corporation with a bag over your head. He was slender and serious and didn't like to look directly at a camera.

Glenda got to New York around three that afternoon and waited outside the offices of CPI. Jeff came out a little after nine-thirty and walked aimlessly for half an hour, winding his way downtown where he stopped in a little cafe.

In the back with a medium coffee, just a little milk, no sugar, he took a few sheets of paper out of his pocket, dense with numbers and marked up with red pen. Glenda ordered a medium coffee, touch of milk, no sugar, and walked up to his table.

"Hello, Mr. Trent. I'm Glenda Hamilton. You know who I am."

She could tell he recognized her right away, and that his first instinct was to run, to bolt for the door. But he wasn't a child anymore.

"I wanted the chance to thank you in person."

"Really. It's not necessary."

"Not necessary? It means everything to us."

"I meant that I don't need you to thank me."

"You just want my husband to have the care he deserves?"

He looked down and stirred his coffee. Glenda did the same. When he was done, he looked up, into her eyes for the first time.

"I don't deserve anything."

"Why not?"

"Do I have to tell you?"

"Yes, you do."

"I think about it every day. I didn't mean to hurt anyone."

"What did you do?"

"I'm sorry."

"What did you do, Jeffrey?"

"I threw something off the overpass, and it hit your car."

"What did you throw?"

"A canned ham."

"Why canned ham?"

"I needed something that weighed eight pounds. For about four months that year Hormel was selling 128-ounce cans. They don't sell them anymore."

"Why did you need to drop ham on the highway?"

"I'd go up there and watch the cars. I could see the highway as a blood vessel. Traffic as blood flow. When you introduce a disruption into that flow . . ."

He put both hands over his face and held them there for nearly half a minute while she got the little packet out of her purse.

"I'll do whatever you say. Should I admit it? Go to the police?"

He'd been barely a teenager when it happened. They wouldn't prosecute on something a juvenile had done more than a decade ago. Would it hurt his career? No. If anything, he'd be lauded for the huge donation and celebrated for acknowledging the childhood mistake.

"Do you remember Vinnie Lane?" Glenda asked.

"Who?"

"The comedian. The TV special? *The Flying Ham* tour?"

"Yes. I remember that."

"Do you remember how he died?"

"Drugs? An OD, wasn't it?"

"I suppose it was." Glenda stirred her drink. "It's impossible to be sure that you've got exactly the right dose to put a man into a coma. Maybe he dies. Maybe he throws up and gets off with a rough weekend. Obviously, I'm not perfect, but I was halfway to a degree in pharmacology when all this happened. What do you weigh, 150?"

"146."

She switched his cup for hers.

"Drink your coffee," she said.

He looked at the cup in front of him but didn't touch it.

"I don't want to die," he said.

"I don't want you to die, either."

Jeff looked down again.

"What do you think he feels?" he asked.

"They tell you a lot of things. You know, different doctors, scientists. But even the people who've woken up can't say for sure what Owen is feeling."

Jeff lifted the cup and drained it. He was still sitting upright when Glenda left the shop.

\*\*\*

Jeff turned back to the columns of data—the most recent lab results. They'd hit a snag; the sort of problem that made you think you were heading the wrong direction. Then in front of him, three small drips of coffee—discrete not continuous. He saw it all. It was counterintuitive, a way to circumvent a deadly blood flow problem without even touching the veins. A completely new idea that would save thousands of lives. He wrote furiously in the margins then on nearby napkins. He thought he had it all mapped clearly enough for smart people to take it forward. Then his head hit the table.

**PRESTON LANG** is a small, honest writer based in Ontario. His short work has appeared in *Thuglit*, *N+1*, **Rock and a Hard Place**, and *Betty Fedora*.

# ROCK AND A HARD PLACE

### SUPPORT US ON  patreon

### LIKE WHAT YOU'RE READING?

YOU CAN HELP US CONTINUE TO PUBLISH THE BEST NOIR AND CRIME FICTION
AROUND BY JOINING OUR PATREON TEAM!

YOU'LL GAIN ACCESS TO BEHIND-THE-SCENE EXTRAS,
INTERVIEWS WITH OUR WRITERS,
SHOUT OUTS IN OUR BOOKS
AND MORE!

SIGN UP TODAY AT PATREON.COM/JOIN/RHPMAG

**NOVEMBER 2023 PROMPT** — The dinner table—a place where families gather, where clients are charmed, where relationships begin and goodbyes are postponed. Breaking bread together is integral to the human experience. The poor do it; world leaders do it. Deals are made. Handshakes exchanged.

So many good things come out of these meetings: memories and progress and high spirits.

We don't want a story about that dinner party. For November, a month that kicks off a bevy of dining-centric holidays, send us your stories of a meal that goes wrong, with dire consequences.

# Pin Bone Stew

## Aidan Shousky

It was a hard thing, watching Jimmy O'Doyle eat. His hands piled food in between his crooked teeth, shoveling scarps of shellfish onto his tongue like a spit-soaked assembly line. He snorted every few seconds and cleared his throat of loose debris. The wet growl that dropped from his mouth sounded like a woodchipper grinding down trash bags filled with jelly. The lump of fat that curled under his chin like a water balloon swelled each time he swallowed.

Riley Byrne, Alfie Sheroka, and Patty McCauley sat around their friend and sipped whiskey. Drinking required little effort, allowing them to focus their collected energy on stuffing down the guilt and agitation that boiled in their stomachs like hot oil. Skins formed on the top of their own bowls of cioppino, thin layers of fish fat and butter sitting stiff like ice on top of a pond. Every time one of them exhaled, the booth that they sat in seemed to constrict. It was like sitting inside the fist of fate, squeezing them all, wringing the cowardice out of their pores like dirty dish water.

"Soup isn't half bad, huh?" Jimmy said as he spooned chunks of cod and mussels into his mouth.

"Can you even taste it?" Patty asked as he sucked down the remainder of his cocktail. He slid out of the booth and walked toward the bar. "Anyone want another one?"

"Maybe bring a bottle over," Alfie said as he lit a cigarette and took a long drag. "I can't taste as much as I used to because of the smokin'. I'd stop, but it's irreversible. That's what my doctor told me."

Jimmy gobbled down a hunk of bread and said, "I started goin' to see this Chinese doctor. He's a one-of-a-kind sorta guy."

"What does that mean?" Riley asked.

"Yous know. Like a character. Just himself."

Alfie shifted his weight so that he was leaning toward his left side. He stirred his spoon around the rim of his bowl and said, "We're all just ourselves, Jimmy. Who isn't themselves?"

"If you weren't yourself, then you'd be somebody else," Riley said.

Patty slid back inside the booth and sat a full bottle of Jameson down in the middle of the table. "Yeah, Jimmy. I gotta agree with everybody else on that," he said, wiggling his gut so that it wasn't pressing into the edge of the table.

"I didn't know I was sittin' with philosophers. It's a common fuckin' expression." Jimmy looked down at his bowl and began eating faster. "You wanna start pickin' apart every little thing that I say? That's fine. But you know what I'm gettin' at."

Riley started to laugh and looked at Alfie. He nodded. Alfie adjusted his posture so that he could reach the .22 Smith & Wesson that was sitting inside of his jacket pocket. Riley said, "That's how I know you're full of shit. You say how we all know it already."

Tension built in Jimmy's jaw. He focused on his breath and said, "When it's true, it's true."

"What makes it true, though? When you think it, say it, or do it?" Riley asked.

Jimmy nearly broke a sweat trying to prevent his hands from shaking. He said, "What does that mean?"

"I think I know what you're gettin' at," Alfie interjected with an inflection as sarcastic as a slide whistle. He leaned forward and sat his elbows on the table, staring over the mountain of flesh and bone that his interlaced hands created. "You can think something. Spend a lot of time thinkin' on it. Seein' every angle. But that doesn't make it a truth.

It's still nothing. You can even say something to somebody. Doesn't make it true. At least not in its entirety. But if you do something..."

"I get it," Patty said. 'When you do the thing, that's set in stone. It happened. It's true. Is that about right?"

"In the ballpark," Riley said.

"Like actions speak louder than words," Alfie said.

Tension gathered in the air like mud. Jimmy continued to eat, keeping his eyes fixed on his bowl. "Almost ruinin' my appetite with all this," he mumbled.

"Didn't stop you though," Patty said.

"When did you get so antsy?" Alfie asked as he pointed to Jimmy's shaky fingers.

"I'm not antsy," Jimmy replied.

Patty smirked and said, "You looked like you were gonna break your teeth you were bitin down so hard. I saw a vein from your head to your fuckin' neck ready to pop."

Alfie slapped his hand on the table and laughed. "He looked scared for a second. Like for real."

Jimmy scooped up a large piece of shrimp and ate it. He followed that with another piece, filling his mouth to capacity. Even with all the food sloshing between his cheeks he spoke. "There's honestly something wrong with yous. Demented-like."

As the others laughed, Riley sat still and let the levity in the air dissipate like smoke. He eyed Jimmy and said, "Some actions speak louder than words. Some."

"I thought we'd moved past this!" Jimmy exclaimed.

"Who said?"

Alfie slid his right hand under the table and rested it on his thigh. Patty blinked, keeping his eyes closed longer each time. He was hoping that he'd get lucky and miss the action.

Jimmy looked at the bowls in front of his friends, still filled to the top. "Not eatin'?" he asked.

"In a bit," Alfie answered.

"Have all you like," Riley said.

Jimmy reached for the loaf of bread that was wrapped in a towel next to the whiskey and ripped off a hunk the size of a softball. He used it to soak up the broth in his bowl. His front teeth tore into the soggy crust like the raw flesh of an animal. "How about we talk about something not fuckin' creepy?" he asked. No one answered, so he continued to swallow bread and stuff panic down his throat. The fear in his blood shut off his brain like a car's ignition.

"You talk louder than you think," Riley said. He looked over to Alfie.

Alfie arched his back and sat up. Jimmy tried to speak, but it was cut off by a gasp and a noise that sounded like a toad wheezing. His hands shot up around his throat and he burst up from his seat like a Jack-in-the-Box.

"What the fuck is that?" Patty said as he exploded out of the booth.

Alfie got up and drew the .22. "Don't fuckin' move, Jimmy."

Riley jumped from his seat and rushed over to Jimmy. He held the man's back and asked, "What the hell are you doin'?"

"Is he fuckin chokin'?" Alfie asked.

Jimmy struggled to stand. His face began to turn red and then purple. He wasn't speaking, but his mouth was open. All he could do was gag and grab at Riley's shirt as he fell to his knees.

Riley smiled and said, "He's choking."

"Do yous know the Hemlock?" Patty asked.

"The fuckin' Hemlock?" Alfie replied.

"Nobody's givin' him the *Heimlich*. Let him choke," Riley ordered. "And put the goddamn gun away."

"This is like a horror movie!" Patty yelled.

Alfie lowered the pistol and watched his friend struggle.

Riley listened to Jimmy gag and said, "Just let it be."

Jimmy collapsed onto the floor. He continued to hold his neck and began to kick his feet. His eyes were bloodshot, and his pupils expanded. The skin on his face turned a dark blue, and as he squirmed on the linoleum, his hands slipped away and fell to his sides, twitching fast like he was being electrocuted.

The other men watched as Riley knelt by Jimmy's face, more life leaving their friend's body with every passing second. He put his hand on his chest and felt the struggle taking place beneath Jimmy's skin, violent spasms making his ribs pulse.

"I hope you can still hear me a bit, pal," Riley whispered. "Before you go, just listen real fast. This is what happens when you forget who your friends are. Hold onto this, wherever you're goin' and know that you're alone."

"Fuckin' snake," Alfie said.

Before Jimmy could look at Riley, his eyes rolled in the back of his head and globs of fish and spit bubbled in the corners of his mouth. He stopped struggling. His fingers curled and his chest settled. For several moments, he was quiet. After a final tremor, he was dead.

"I can't believe that just fuckin' happened," Patty said.

"Sometimes, God gives you a break," Riley added.

Alfie took a long look at Jimmy's face and said, "Yeah, I don't know if God makes people choke. I could be wrong, but I doubt it."

"That was wild," Patty said. "It was . . . Is he actually dead?"

Alfie walked closer to Jimmy's body and stomped his foot. The body just jiggled. "Yeah. He's definitely gone."

"Christ, he went down quick," Patty exclaimed.

"I feel pretty unsatisfied," Alfie mumbled.

"Yeah. Lot of build up for that," Riley added.

"What do you we do with him now?" Patty asked.

Riley stood up and circled the body. Alfie and Patty moved toward the bar and sat on the empty stools. No one said it out loud, but all three men were thinking the same thing. Jimmy's sloppy habits and glutinous ways saved them the anguish that comes with murdering a life-long companion. It took dying for him to finally do something decent for somebody other than himself.

"I lined my trunk already," Patty said. "Give me two seconds and I'll back down the alley."

"No. We don't need that now," Riley responded.

"Well, I'd at least like to get him up off my floor. He's probably sitting in his own shit."

Alfie lit a cigarette and walked back over to the table. His fingers grazed the handle of a spoon that was submerged under the thin red broth in Jimmy's bowl. He saw the large chunks of cod and squid and said, "Who cooked this?"

"I got it from the Italian market. The fish place," Patty said.

"Cut up all this shit kinda big, huh?"

"That's why I didn't touch it. Half of that probably isn't cooked," Riley said. He got up and looked into the bowl that Alfie was examining.

"I found a pin bone in mine," Patty said as he got up from the stool and joined his friends. "Once I felt that in between my teeth, I was done with it." He looked over his shoulder at Jimmy's body, noticing the look that was frozen on his face. The eyes were dilated and bloodshot. The mouth hung open like he was trying to scream.

"This is gonna sound dumb, but I feel bad for him," said Patty.

Alfie strolled past him, behind the bar to grab a beer. "I'm not sure I know why."

Riley was staring at his own shirt sleeve and didn't even seem to hear either man.

Patty stood over Jimmy's body and said, "If you just would've shot him, I'd be okay with that. It's what he deserved and all. But going like this, that's just a friend dyin'. Does that make sense?"

"No. I can't say it does," Alfie said.

Patty turned around and looked at Riley. "What do you think?" he asked.

"About what?" Riley replied.

"My theory."

Riley raised his arm, holding the end of his sleeve toward the overhead lights, and said, "Jimmy stained my shirt. Spit on my sleeve or something." He moved toward the bar, stepping over the body like it was a piece of chewed gum.

"You never said what to do with him," Alfie muttered.

"Call 911," Riley said. "But first, get me some club soda. I gotta save this shirt."

**AIDAN SHOUSKY** was born and raised in North Philadelphia where he worked part-time as an art teacher and private investigator. He graduated from Temple University with a bachelor's degree in English and Film. While at the university, he was a member of Philadelphia Young Playwrights. He currently lives in Saint Paul, MN and works as an editorial assistant.

**DECEMBER 2023 PROMPT** — To celebrate the season of light and gift-giving, send us your stories of gifts, given or received, wanted and unwanted, and the wreckage they leave in their wake.

Happy Holidays, Stone's Throw Family!

# Pay the Ferryman

## Libby Cudmore

Hen wondered if she would miss the taste of vending machine coffee. Every afternoon the ritual was the same: two sugars, two non-dairy creamers, take the cup to her husband's room and tell him about her day. She wished there was a barista, a friendly face to recognize her amidst so much machinery. The attendants were not supposed to be friendly with the clients. Everything at the Slumbr Center was purely transactional. No one could be accused of favors or favorites. Even after six months, the attendants refused to acknowledge her beyond a head nod when they came to check Robert's vitals. Always the same. He was still alive. And he would stay that way until she could come up with $250,000.

\*\*\*

Hen's mother died sick and screaming in her bed. She was eight when her mom began vomiting blood, 10 when she finally succumbed to the war inside her body. By contrast, when her father drunkenly shot himself in the garage six months later, she imagined he hadn't felt a thing. That was as close to a peaceful death as she knew.

***

When visiting hours were over, Hen threw out her empty coffee cup and got in her car. She drove two towns over to the lone gas station that still had an attendant. Most of them were automated now; a few gas pumps and a room-sized vending machine where you could order Slim Jims or Diet Cokes or No-Doze for the road. She was sick of machines. She needed to see a person.

She found a new use for the nylons she'd put in the back of the drawer when Robert got sick. She still had her father's revolver – the rifle he'd put in his mouth was incinerated long ago as evidence. She took these both into the store as soon as she saw the last customer leave, when she was sure no one else was inside.

"Everything you have in the register," she said, "and no one gets hurt."

***

When Robert got sick, the caseworker at the hospital told them about Slumbr. When he was ready, Denise explained, they would put him into a medicated sleep so Hen could say her goodbyes at her own pace. No screaming. No blood or chest pains, no suffocating as fluid filled his lungs. A perfect death, as deaths go. They signed the form, picked a date, and spent one last evening together. They went to that Michelin-starred restaurant they always said they'd try. They held hands at the movies. He fell asleep in her arms, and she lay awake, stroking his hair, savoring his scent, wondering how she would put her life back together without him. In the morning, they drove to the Slumbr Center, and held hands as his eyes closed and his breathing relaxed.

That was five months ago.

What Denise did not tell her was the cost. To turn the machines off was $500,000, a bargain, really, for control over death. Their insurance would pay half, but that left her on the hook for the rest of it. If she didn't pay the $250,000 in six months, the cost would double. Then double that at the end of the year.

She'd tried GoFundMe, spaghetti dinners and raffles. Her friends and his co-workers had given what they could, but they had spouses and families, too. She was $5,000 short. She might as well have been $250,000 short. There was nothing left to pawn, nothing left to sell. She didn't have a choice.

The first time she robbed a store, she threw up with nerves. Her hands trembled on the revolver as she told the teenage clerk to put the money in the bag. He didn't seem threatened. The store had insurance, after all, and it was only $43. In the morning, he would tell his friends of his bravery in the face of danger. The gun wasn't even loaded. She was too afraid she might actually have to use it.

***

Five down.

Hen had carefully mapped her targets. 50 miles or less in radius; liquor stores, gas stations, small groceries. The liquor stores always had the most cash, but they were used to hold-ups, and often had cameras. There were more gas stations on her list, but they emptied the register every time they hit $50. The food co-ops were a sweet middle ground; they were too passive to fight back, even if sometimes they only had $25 in cash. Once, the cashier even offered her a scone. *Eat*, she'd said. *You wouldn't have to do this if someone took care of you.* She had tears in her eyes as she took the scone and $200 from the register. She wished she could explain why she was doing this, that she wasn't a bad person, that she was just trying to take care of someone she loved. The scone was the best she'd ever had, a three-cheese blend with almond flour, nutty and savory all at once. She wished she could go back for another.

It wasn't worth the risk. The papers reported the robberies in small columns, but none of them ever made the connection between the towns. That's where the 50-mile radius was important.

She frowned at the list. There were no other stores to hit. She was $500 short. In another week, her rent would be due. Three days after that, the electric. She was almost out of cup noodles and lentils. Everything she could spare was gone; she was in a sleeping bag on the floor, watching TV on her phone with internet she pirated from the McDonald's next door. She needed one big score, like they said in heist movies. A casino, or the mob, or an armored car.

Or a bank.

\*\*\*

The Neighbors Bank branch near her house had plenty of cameras and a retired cop as a guard. She assumed there was an under-the-counter button system to alert the cops. She strolled through the lobby, picking up a pamphlet and smiling at the clerk so as not to look suspicious. She and Robert had always used Wilshire Bank, the original location of what would grow to be a regional chain. In spite of their name, Neighbors Bank had been aggressive in pushing out other operations, opening branches on all four sides of town. *A bank you can walk to*, their advertisements read. *That's a good Neighbor*. She hated those advertisements. They even offered savings accounts for Slumbr. The pamphlet in her hand featured a smiling elderly couple walking through a lush fall scene. *Put some aside for peace of mind*, the copy read. She had to fight the urge to rip it to pieces right there. A bank job just wasn't possible. There were too many variables, too many witnesses. She'd have to find the $500 elsewhere.

Then she noticed the ATM.

The ATM was in the vestibule outside of the lobby. There were only two cameras, one on the machine itself and one off to the side. A hoodie would obscure her face from the one, and the stocking she wore for the other robberies would obscure her face further. She could arrive after the bank closed and before the bars opened and wait for some pre-gamed college student to come collect some cash for his tab. She could put her gun in his back and demand he withdraw $500, the limit. The next morning she could go to the Slumbr Center, pay Robert's bill and kiss him goodbye one last time. It was fail-proof. And even if she did get caught in the end, what did it matter? Prison might be an upgrade to the way she was living now.

\*\*\*

Hen didn't get vending machine coffee this time. Didn't want to waste her hard-earned cash, not when she was this close to paying off his debt. "I've almost got the money," she said, patting Robert's hand. "You'll be out of here soon. I promise."

She tried to imagine what it would feel like to finally say goodbye. Slumbr had lived up to its promise. She got more time with her husband. There was never going to be enough of it. 35 years of marriage. They'd built a home, first in a basement apartment, then in the Cape Cod-style she sold at far below cost three months ago, to a smirking woman who stripped out all Robert's woodwork and replaced it with cheap décor designed to impress AirBnB guests. Hen and Robert had laughed together. They'd cried together through three miscarriages. They traveled to Tokyo and Prague, they were going to spend their retirement years in a RV crossing the country. In the end, they both knew one of them would have to go on without the other. That time was coming up soon. She had to be ready. She couldn't afford not to be.

\*\*\*

Hen waited. It was nearly midnight. Plenty of people had come through the ATM, but they had come in groups. It was too risky to try and hold up three or four young men. There was a cluster of girls, in tube dresses and sweatshirts and sneakers, but they didn't go inside. She couldn't help but smile. When she was that age, she never had to pay for drinks either.

A man came up the street, away from the bars. He threw down his cigarette, took out his wallet, and went inside. She followed him and scanned her card backwards, once, twice, a third time. She pounded on the door, smiled, and shook her head. "I'm sorry," she said. "I think something's wrong with the magnetic strip."

"They're more trouble than they're worth, aren't they?" he said. There was cheap beer on his breath. "But I guess that's what we get for coming after closing. Ladies first."

"Oh no," she said, reaching into her purse and wrapping her hand around the gun. "You go ahead."

He turned his back to her. She eased the gun out of her bag and stuck it in his back. "$500," she said, letting all the honey drip from her voice.

He didn't flinch. He didn't press any buttons. Then he turned around and punched her. She fell, smashing her back on a sharp corner of the wall. The gun clattered to the floor. He put his hand through the door, triggering the alarm. "You think you can rob me?" he screamed, climbing on top of her. "You think you can steal from me?"

He grabbed the gun. She tried to run, grabbing for the door handle and pushing with everything she had until it gave. She fell on her knees on the sidewalk outside. She couldn't breathe. It wasn't until she saw the blood pooling beneath her that she realized she had been shot.

Bystanders swarmed from cars and bars. Someone restrained her assailant; she heard him insist she tried to rob him. *It was a good thing I didn't wear my stocking*, she thought. It would have given her away instantly. A man laid her out flat, applying pressure to the wound. Every breath hurt, fire and ice wracking her body. Blood spurted up through his fingers. She could hear shouting and sirens in the distance. Everything was too bright. She closed her eyes.

*Until death do us part.*

If there was no one to pay the cost, Robert's machine would be unplugged. He would finally get to die. He wouldn't know that he was alone, wouldn't know that she had predeceased him by hours. Would they meet in the afterlife? Would their lawyer retrieve her body from the city morgue so they could be buried side by side, as they dictated in their wills? There wasn't time to find out. She couldn't wait another minute.

She swatted the man's hand away. She willed her heart to beat harder, to pump out as much blood as she could before the ambulance arrived. It wasn't the most honorable death. It wasn't the most peaceful death.

But it was hers.

And it was free.

**LIBBY CUDMORE** (Twitter: @LibbyCudmore) is the Shamus-winning author of *Negative Girl* (Datura 2024) and *The Big Rewind* (William Morrow 2016.) She is a frequent contributor to *Ellery Queen Mystery Magazine* and her stories have been published in *Tough, The Dark, Monkeybicycle, Had, Reckon Review* and others.

# EDITORIAL BIOGRAPHIES

**R.D. SULLIVAN** (*Stone's Throw* Editor; Twitter: @_TheRussian) is a writer of fiction, comedy, and letters to the editor. Her work can be found at *Fireside Fiction Magazine*, *Shotgun Honey*, and *Tough*, as well as in the *Killing Malmon* and *Murder-A-Go-Go's* anthologies. She now lives in North Carolina with her kiddo and mutts, and is an aspiring woodland hermit. You can track her down over at govneh.com.

**ROGER NOKES** (RHP Editor-in-Chief; Twitter: @McCaffery_write) writes fiction under the pseudonym Stanton McCaffrey. His short stories have been featured in *Dark Yonder*, *Mystery Magazine*, *Guilty*, *Mystery Tribune*, *Vautrin*, *Shotgun Honey*, and more. He has published two novels: *Into the Ocean*; and *Neighborhood of Dead Ends*.

**ALBERT TUCHER** (Contributing Editor; Twitter: @AlbertTucher) is the creator of prostitute Diana Andrews, who has appeared in more than 100 hardboiled stories in venues including *The Best American Mystery Stories 2010*. Her first longer case, the novella *The Same Mistake Twice*, was published in 2013. In 2017 Albert Tucher launched a second series set on the Big Island of Hawaii, in which *Pele's Prerogative* is the latest entry. He is a past president of the Mystery

Writers of America NY Chapter. He lives in New Jersey, and loves NJ Turnpike jokes.

**JAY BUTKOWSKI** (Managing Editor; Twitter: @jtbutkowski) is a writer of fiction, an eater of tacos and an amateur pizzaiolo who lives in New Jersey. His stories have appeared in online and print publications, including *Shotgun Honey*, *Yellow Mama*, *All Due Respect*, *Dark Yonder*, and *Vautrin*, among others. He is a founding editor at **Rock and a Hard Place Press**, an independent publisher chronicling "bad decisions and desperate people." He's also a father of twins, a newlywed husband, and a middling pancake chef.

**PAUL J. GARTH** (Associate Editor; Twitter: @PauljGarth) is an editor for **Rock and a Hard Place Press**. His short fiction has been published in *Thuglit*, *Tough*, *Needle: A Magazine of Noir*, *Plots with Guns*, *Crime Factory*, ***Rock and a Hard Place Magazine***, and several other anthologies and web magazines. His novella, *The Low White Plain*, part of the "A Grifter's Song" series, was released in June 2022. He lives and writes in Nebraska, where he lives with his family.

**ROB D. SMITH** (Associate Editor; Twitter: @RobSmith3) is a common man attempting to write uncommon fiction in Louisville, KY. His work has appeared in *Apex Magazine*, *Shotgun Honey*, *The Arcanist*, *Pyre Magazine*, *Thriller Magazine*, *Bristol Noir*, ***Rock and a Hard Place Magazine***, *Tough*, *Vautrin*, and several other crime, horror, and speculative anthologies and online magazines. Find more about him at https://robdsmith.carrd.co/.

Made in the USA
Middletown, DE
24 July 2024